THE WRATH OF THE KING

THE WRATH
OF
THE KING

by WALTER C. UTT

PACIFIC PRESS PUBLISHING ASSOCIATION

Mountain View, California   Oshawa, Ontario

To My Father and Mother

Library of Congress Catalog Card No. 66-29028

The story of the Huguenots reads like a continuation of Hebrews, chapter eleven. These devout Protestants combined faith and works in heroic proportions. They were famed for both their religious zeal and their diligence in business. In the severe persecutions to which they were subjected, some abandoned their religion to save their lives and property. But other thousands died or rotted in dungeons or galleys "that they might obtain a better resurrection." Many escaped to the Low Countries, England, and America, leaving their homeland the poorer for their exit.

The Huguenots loved the Scriptures, and liberally sprinkled their daily conversation with Biblical allusions. They studied the book of Revelation and knew themselves to be a people of prophecy. They referred, for example, to their beloved country, in its apostate condition, as "spiritual Egypt." Revelation 11:8. The state church they often called "the Scarlet Woman." Revelation 17:4. Their rural environment in southern France they denominated the "wilderness" or "desert" to which the virtuous woman fled. Revelation 12:14-17

The author of this volume, a devoted Francophile, has immersed himself in books on French history for thirty years. He has traveled in France and done research in the Huguenot library in Paris. He has delved into the quarterly *Bulletin de la Société de l'Histoire du Protestantisme Français* from its 1896 issues onward. For additional background material he has used such sources as *The Huguenots and the Revocation of the Edict of Nantes*, by Baird; *History of the Edict of Nantes*, by Benoit; *Torments of French Protestant Slaves*, by Arber; and some seventy other volumes. He is conversant with French lore and customs, especially those of the Huguenots—their cities and streets, their churches and manner of worship, their homes and family life, their kings and clergymen, their sufferings and hardships, their journeys and escapes.

As students in his college history classes have often testified, the author is unusually gifted in the art of making history come alive. In this volume, rather than exposing the dry bones of historical names and dates before a jaded and possibly somnolent reader, the author has clothed with flesh the skeleton of fact as he weaves the narrative of a typical Huguenot family and of an army officer forced to choose between allegiance to his king and loyalty to his God. The incidents related are true ones, substantiated by existing historical records.

The issues the Huguenots faced are those which Christ's followers in other times and places have had to meet: Can Christians outwardly observe the commands of an idolatrous ruler, while in mind and conscience they cling to their faith? When persecuted, should Christians defend themselves if they are able, meeting violence with violence? When is it the part of wisdom to flee the persecutor, and when is it cowardice?

Someday we as individual Christians may have to answer the greatest question of all: Am I willing to surrender possessions, even life itself, to obey God rather than men? May the reader be better enabled rightly to answer this great question, as he more thoroughly acquaints himself with the inspiring epic of the Huguenots.

THE PUBLISHERS.

CHAPTER 1

I

THE tall man in a discolored riding cloak drew his big bay horse to a sudden stop and dismounted.

"Ah! A new and splendid victory for the dragoons," he remarked acidly.

A soldier wearing the red coat of the dragoons turned, a black scowl on his leathery, unshaven face.

"Who asked you—?" he began furiously.

Meanwhile the dragoon was holding a boy firmly by the collar, as the boy industriously kicked at his tormentor's shins. But the boy was handicapped by the tall, heavy riding boots of the soldier, and by the fact that the latter held him clear of the ground. Eventually the dragoon dropped the boy to terra firma, but kept a firm grip on his collar.

"I simply asked this whelp where the priest lived, and he insulted me—sir." He added the last reluctantly, as he suddenly recognized an infantry officer's gray uniform under the faded riding cloak.

The officer and the dragoon now faced each other. The tanned and handsome officer stood a head taller than the stocky soldier. The officer's firm jaw and general air of competence suggested to the observer that he was a career man and not one of those fops from the Versailles ballrooms.

"And where are your manners, boy?" asked the officer severely, for the youngster was well dressed.

A knot of spectators gathered in the littered, unpaved street of the southern French town of Saint Martin. A few feet away stood a saddled horse belonging to the dragoon, and a coach, covered with yellow road dust, its leather curtains drawn in spite of the warm spring weather. A coachman nodded on the box.

The boy answered boldly. "When he asked for the priest, I asked him if he wore his red coat because he was in the service of the Scar-

1

let Woman." His eyes were a trifle too close together for him to be considered good-looking, and his teeth were prominent; but he fairly radiated keenness and energy.

"You see!" cried the dragoon. "The rascal is one of these pestilential heretics. In the coach yonder is the subdelegate of this province who comes to this town to deal with these brazen folk. I'd say it's high time!"

"Well, young man," said the officer to the boy, "you see you do the people of the Reform no service giving out your sauce in this fashion. Give this gentleman his directions and crave his pardon."

The boy obeyed quickly and insincerely apologized. The soldier released him. The officer then spoke with some sarcasm:

"It appears a little strange that French soldiers have no better employment than to harass peaceable folk whose only offense is their religion."

The dragoon averted his gaze a little from the piercing black eyes. "As you know, sir," he said, "there isn't much doing on the frontiers these days; but playing nursemaid to these civilians," and he gestured toward the coach, "is better than sleeping in wet straw or stealing chickens. Besides, something has to be done about these Huguenots —two religions in a kingdom is as unreasonable as two kings." He straightened his drooping tasseled cap. "The intendant is very zealous of late against the heretics, and we are here to stir up the local people to make things interesting for those who won't change their religion."

A shadow crossed the officer's face, and he shrugged.

"The king has turned devout, you know," persisted the dragoon, "so maybe this is a good time to see what makes these heretics think they are better than other folk." He hesitated. "Well, it won't be the first time soldiers have played at missionary."

"Your zeal does you credit, but then I fancy a dragoon has sins enough to atone for."

The dragoon had no time to reply, for a bewigged head thrust itself through the coach curtain.

"Monsieur wishes to know what is the reason for the delay," it said crossly.

"I was obtaining directions," the dragoon explained. "We are almost there." He turned to mount his horse. "No offense, sir, I hope," he said pausing. "I am Dupin of the Dauphin's Regiment, and sixteen years in his majesty's service." He saluted.

2

"Gandon, major in the Regiment of Maine," replied the officer courteously as he returned the salute.

The coach and dragoon moved on, and the idlers began to disperse. The officer turned to the boy, who had been gazing up at him in open-mouthed admiration.

"Without letting that tongue of yours get away again, young man, can you tell me where I might find Monsieur Cortot, who was a tax farmer, I believe, when I was here ten years ago?"

"He's my father," exclaimed the boy.

"Good! You can show me the way. Your father and mine were friends long ago."

"Yes, monsieur, but monsieur will not need to mention this affair of the dragoon? Thank you, monsieur! Just come this way."

II

SOMEWHAT to his surprise, Armand de Gandon discovered that he was enjoying the long evening worship of the Cortot family. It had been years since he had been a part of such a gathering, and as Isaac Cortot launched into the third Scripture passage, Armand recalled some of the warmth and security he had felt as a boy by the glow of other evening fires, before his mother died and he and his father had gone away to the wars.

He marveled at the readiness with which Monsieur and Madame Cortot had welcomed him, as if he had been a visiting angel passing through Saint Martin rather than a travel-stained infantry officer who had not seen them since he was a boy in his teens. He recalled with awe the dinner, the endless platters of boiled and roasted meats, the soups, the sweetmeats. It must have been the finest table in town. His father's old comrade must be a most substantial citizen, for the establishment combined Huguenot simplicity with elegance.

Digesting comfortably in the chimney corner, Armand watched the firelight play about the features of his friends. Monsieur Cortot, in blue serge and silver buckles, looked the part of retired civil servant to perfection. With his spectacles down his nose, he leaned into the light of the candelabra on the table as he read a chapter in Isaiah. He was ruddy, of average height but more than average girth. At the moment he was wearing his hat, but Armand had noticed that his hair was sparse and grizzled.

A glance at Madame Cortot, in her dark gown and her white cap and apron, sitting primly in a high-backed settle beside her husband, was confirmation that she fitted perfectly in these surroundings. Even to the Ten Commandments hanging on the parlor wall behind her head and the motto incised over the huge fireplace—"Who builds not the house in the Lord builds in vain." Her calm eye and assured manner as she sat with her embroidery needles temporarily idle in her lap, spoke of the competent manager, the plump and utterly respectable queen of a provincial domain.

Armand was conscious that his attention had wandered from the reading. His slightly guilty gaze swept quickly over the four children. They were dark, and except for the boy Alexandre, rather handsome. Louis and Louise, the shy and solemn twins, sat on stools one on each side of their mother. They might be seven or eight, he guessed. He sympathized with them in their bashfulness. He recalled how he, too, as youngest at the table, had had to offer grace before company. He had probably not been any more audible than Louis had been this evening. The twins had just begun to warm to him a little during the dessert course. Like all Huguenot children, they had probably been warned against strangers ever since they could remember. The gleaming gold braid, gilt buttons, and bright red cuffs of his uniform must have been a new sight at this quiet table. He would have to make special efforts to win their confidence.

There was no problem getting aquainted with Alexandre, now sitting beside him in the chimney corner. The boy obviously had more energy than he knew what to do with anyway. He could not keep his eyes off the officer's uniform, and except for the strong opinion held by Huguenots that children were to be modest in the presence of their elders, Armand felt certain the boy would have asked to try on the hat and heft the sword. With his toe Alexandre was digging absently at the furry underside of a gray kitten sprawled on the flagstones—until the movement caught the attention of his little brother. And that, in turn, brought a stern glance from his mother.

The soldier found his roving eye resting longest on the pretty, thoughtful face of Madeleine, the tall and graceful eldest daughter of the house. Her eyes fastened on her father, her hands folded quietly in her lap, she seemed unaware of his scrutiny. The candlelight glinted on her shoulder-length dark hair, and her white cap and *fichu** seemed the whiter for the contrast. In this poor light he could not see her eyes, but at the dinner table he had noticed they were a striking shade of blue—more violet in fact than blue—and set off by long lashes. For all her demure manner, Armand noticed there could be a blue spark in those eyes, as when at the table she had used a sisterly elbow to cut off a talkative twelve-year-old brother.

With a pang he realized that his years of hard work and the genteel poverty of a career officer had not given him much opportunity to think seriously along such lines. There had certainly been nothing like this in any garrison town he knew! He wondered what bucolic notable had bespoken this latter-day Esther. She certainly must have been promised, for she must be sixteen or seventeen at least. And where, he asked himself, did she get her graceful slimness? Both her parents looked like heavily built folk.

Behind Madeleine, in the shadows, sat three or four servants. Armand recalled vaguely that there had been at least two other children in the family at the time of his earlier visit. One must have been lost young, and there had been a boy his own age he remembered more clearly. That one had died for the king in the Low Countries. It must be his portrait, done in charcoal by some itinerant artist, on the mantel between the Nevers figurines.

The voice of his host seemed dim in the distance. The words of the prophet Isaiah rolled over him. He was in a trance, far from the dangerous world outside where greed, ambition, and hatred played unchecked. Here was an island of peace and trust. Armand felt lifted out of time and reality. This was the very anteroom of heaven.

III

FATHER CHABERT, priest in Saint Martin, settled himself at his polished ebony table, interlaced his fingers over his round stomach, and beamed in high good humor at his guest, a hawk-faced young man in a rust-colored suit, with Venetian lace at throat and cuffs, and a long glossy black wig. The priest's chubby face was shining with sweat and anticipation. Dust specks glittered and danced in the shaft of sunlight pouring in through the open windows of the pastoral parlor. From the garden rose the hum of insects and the desultory conversation of birds.

*An ornamental three-cornered cape.

"The local Huguenots cling tenaciously to the abominable blasphemies of Calvin," the priest explained, "and pretend a meekness of spirit which is belied by the obstinacy with which they resist the conviction of the True Faith and the entreaties of His Gracious Majesty."

The visitor stifled a yawn. It promised to be a difficult afternoon. Charles Marie Joseph de Beausejour, subdelegate to the intendant of the province, had come at last in answer to repeated calls to take stock of the situation at Saint Martin. Though one must pretend a certain respect for the cloth, the official found it difficult to conceal his antipathy for this balding little priest perched there so eagerly in his big carved chair. The reflected glare from the table top hurt the official's eyes, and there was the racket of those insects and birds. He felt a dull resentment at being trapped here in this overheated rural desert.

The priest droned on: "While I would not in any way criticize the work of my predecessor in this parish (God rest his soul), yet the laxity here must have passed belief. 'Tis even said that Father Forbin thought it blasphemy to compel an unconvinced person to assist at mass!" He paused expectantly, but the bored official made no effort to answer.

"It has been well nigh a quarter of a century since His Gracious Majesty has heeded the appeals of the clergy and has begun to deal stringently with the menace of the Pretended Reformed Religion." He clenched his fist. "I have, of course, done what I could to see that the laws are obeyed, but my humble efforts have been without fruit; yes, virtually without fruit. There are only a few hundred of these P.R.R. openly practicing here, but much of the town was once so—even the mayor and the city council are mostly New Catholics—and they make endless difficulties for me—quibbles, arrant nonsense."

Father Chabert then sketched in a few thousand well chosen words a history of the religious troubles of the preceding 150 years.

"What a wearisome fellow," thought the subdelegate. "He never even stops to draw breath!"

". . . The hydra of heresy must be crushed, my lord. Its heads multiply when there is paltering with error. Its venom has infected the blood of our land, and we see the dread consequences on every side. We soldiers of the First Estate, defenders of the True Faith in

6

the very forefront of the battle, as it were, never cease our prayers for the enlightenment of His Majesty. We count ourselves favored, imperfect vessels though we are, that he so vigorously prosecutes the cause of the Faith throughout the realm—"

De Beausejour interrupted in sudden desperation: "I pray you, my good Father, have done with this sermon and let us get on with the business!"

Suddenly aware of the sour look on his auditor's face, the curé halted the speech in mid flight.

"The intendant has your letter," said the official, hastily exploiting his advantage, "and authorizes me to take whatever steps may be necessary to raze the Huguenot temple. However, he is anxious that all the legal formalities be observed, and has instructed me to examine all the evidence carefully. He would be *most* annoyed if ill-considered action gave the Pretended Reformed an opportunity to complain at court through their representative."

"Oh, most assuredly, most assuredly!"

De Beausejour shifted in his chair and raised a languid, white hand. "What are your proofs that the P.R.R. have violated the law?" Too late he realized he had restored the initiative to the priest, whose explanations, he feared, might start well back of Noah.

But this time the curé got to the point: "Surely I do not need to refresh monsieur's memory as to the edict of 1679 which provides that if the heretics allow a New Convert to attend their services, their building is to be destroyed and the pastor is liable to public penance, the *amende honorable,** as well as fine and banishment if His Majesty please."

He dropped his eyes modestly. "To carry it out, I found a former lackey, somewhat decayed in his estate and willing to accept the customary payment to adjure the Calvinistic delusion." His little eyes sparkled, and he grinned slyly.

He paused, that the deadly simplicity of his scheme might be fully appreciated.

"You have witnesses to this happy 'coincidence'—the backsliding of this lackey?"

Father Chabert thumbed through a sheaf of papers:

"We have here his abjuration under date of June 15, 1683," he presently announced, "and here are the sworn statements—all nota-

*A humiliating confession of guilt, with public apology.

7

rized, all dated the first of last month—of my witnesses who saw him at the Huguenot services."

The subdelegate accepted the papers and glanced at them listlessly.

"I'll authorize your mayor then," said he, "to proceed with the closing of the temple. Doubtless he can arrange for the labor if the heretics don't wish to demolish it themselves." His chair squealed as he pushed it back. "My secretary can draw up the papers. I'll call on the P.R.R. minister this afternoon."

The curate's face fell. Apparently he had hoped for this pleasure himself.

"Well," he resumed a little grumpily, "there are also other ways in which the pride of the heretics should be humbled. There is the cross in honor of Our Saviour and Redeemer Jesus Christ which should be raised on the site of their temple. And may I call to your attention the edict of 1681 which provides that the children of the P.R.R. above the age of seven who are converted, or who evince a desire for conversion, may be placed for instruction in the Houses for New Catholics. His Majesty's efforts in behalf of these unfortunate children are now four years old and nothing has been done yet in this city.

"I have here," he continued, rummaging in his papers, "a list of the Pretended Reformed Religion families of the town. I could send it to the bishop, but it might save time in such an important matter if you could examine it, in the room of the intendant, so to speak. Now that we will soon have a House for New Catholics on the outskirts of town, I would earnestly bespeak the cooperation of the civil authorities to fill it."

"You have the authority already, do you not?"

"Assuredly we could fill the house, and the one for boys down country also, yes, several times over. But it's a matter of funds, monsieur." He eyed his adversary expectantly. "Voluntary contributions are but a trickle, sir, and the mayor and the council are stingy in the extreme—they elevate cheeseparing to an art. You know how these merchants behave when there is a new religious house coming to their town! The work of conversion must, I fear, rest largely on the royal bounty."

"You churchmen are always putting the cart before the horse," yawned de Beausejour. "The law provides for the upkeep of such

8

inmates by their parents according to their means. Confine your recruiting to those able to pay their own way. The intendant has a thousand parishes plaguing him with ten thousand silly requests and squabbles, all of them expensive. Public revenues can't be called on for everything, you know."

"But, monsieur," the priest cried, his chins shaking indignantly, "is there *any* work of greater importance than to wrest these children from the very jaws of hell? The old are almost beyond redemption; the young may still be persuaded. The Houses for New Catholics make devoted subjects for His Majesty from the children of his enemies. From bad trees, good fruit! It would seem that for this divine work of pacification, this plucking of brands from the burning, as it were, that funds might be spared—"

"The houses should support themselves," interrupted de Beausejour stubbornly. He noted the disappointment on the priest's face and hurried on. Best not antagonize these zealots too far. "The work of conversion is dear to all our hearts, but taxes come hard this year, and we must go slowly. Now, if no further requests are made on the treasury, I'm sure the intendant will be happy to assist you to take as many children as the Houses can accommodate." He rubbed his chin thoughtfully. "But stay within the law in this matter also. You are able to get all these children to ask for instruction?"

The priest brightened somewhat.

"That's no trouble. Well, not much, anyway. These children are often discreet beyond their years, but sometimes the younger ones will say 'Hail Mary' for a sweet or gewgaw. Or if it is reported that an older child has admired the magnificence of an altar or a procession, we are able to construe such a favorable remark as a request for instruction, as the law is interpreted nowadays. We must use care, for these people are to the last degree opinionated and may flee the country if they suspect we are after their children.

"But there will be no disturbance, my lord.

"Now this is my list as of last month. I have arranged the P.R.R. families by streets, with the name and age of each child. It was much work, I can tell you," he added complacently. "Some we wouldn't want, it's true. Too young or sickly for good instruction, for example."

The official studied the sheets, crackling the stiff paper as he looked through them.

"Well," said de Beausejour at length, "let's check the ones who can be supported by their parents. Perhaps some other likely ones may be taken also if the charges on the wealthy are placed high enough."

The priest beamed. "And might there not also be royal pensions for the poor at a later date, perhaps?" He moved closer so he could follow the list.

"I'm not paid to foretell the future," said de Beausejour sourly. "Let us do it my way for now."

"Certainly, monsieur, certainly," agreed Father Chabert quickly.

The subdelegate leaned back as the priest began to read the list. The secretary silently dipped a quill in the inkwell and made notations in the margin of his copy as dictated by his master.

"On the Rue de Montauban," began the priest, "we have the following: 'Isaac Cortot, bourgeois. Four children: Madeleine, 16; Alexandre, 12; Louis and Louise, 7.' He is the richest heretic in town and owns lands besides. He was in the controller's office until the Huguenot tax officials were dismissed. The children are all sturdy, and he can certainly support them."

"Take them all," dictated the subdelegate with his eyes closed. The secretary's pen scratched briefly.

"On the same street, 'Emile Robert, ironmonger. Three children: Denise, 10; Emile, 7; Rebekah, 3.'"

"Eh, that's too young. Take Denise and Emile."

"On the same street, 'Jean Delzers, former bookseller. Five children: Samuel, 15; Jean, 14; Georges, 12; Hannah, 10; Gaspard, 9. He is poor, the law not permitting him to follow his trade of late, but the children are healthy."

"They would be public charges," commented the official. "Write, 'Do not take unless later vacancies.'"

Father Chabert looked pained but continued to read:

"'Gabriel Piel, weaver, on the Street of the Three Lions—'" He broke off. "This family is reported to have gone into foreign parts. It is hard to keep such a list up to date," he added apologetically. "They fly from here in such stealth."

The secretary noted in the margin, "Disappeared."

"Also in the same street, 'Jules Pinet, tanner. Two children: Olivier, 9; Henri, 8.' Olivier is sickly. The father is reputed to do a good business."

"Leave Olivier—"

10

IV

MONSIEUR CORTOT had finished his chapter and had launched into the final prayer of the evening when there came a heavy rapping at the front door. The worshipers stirred uneasily on their knees, but the petitioner did not falter or shorten his prayer. When he had finished, one of the maids slipped away to unbar the door. While the group waited in some apprehension, the kitten rose and stretched and lay down farther away from Alexandre.

Three solemn men were ushered into the room. Everyone rose, the men removing their hats, the ladies curtsying.

"Good evening, pastor," said Cortot heartily as he bowed over the hand of the first of the newcomers. "What brings you out at this time of day?"

"Nothing good, you may be sure," replied Pastor Merson with a thin smile. He bowed again to the rest of the company. "I would not lightly interrupt the devotions of my chief elder. I crave your pardon until I may make explanations."

Madame Cortot made polite deprecatory noises, and the host proceeded with the introductions:

"Brethren," he began, "I have the honor to present to you Henri Armand, the Sieur de Gandon, the son of my late friend and brother in the Religion, Michel de Gandon. The elder Gandon and I served together—back in the fifties, it was—under the illustrious Schomberg when our Protestant marshal was but a general.

"And these gentlemen, Armand, are our good pastor, Jean Merson, his nephew Mathieu Bertrand, our schoolteacher and catechist here in Saint Martin, and this is our head deacon, Brother Estienne Lenotre."

The pastor offered Armand his hand with a kindly smile.

"We are honored, brother, that you have come among us."

Armand bowed in his turn, taking in the whole group and dropping his eyes as was mannerly when conversing with strangers. He was uncomfortably conscious of the contrast between his uniform and the sober hues worn by the visitors. He saw the pastor as a slight man in his early forties, in a black clerical mantle, wide-brimmed beaver hat, spotless white collar, and short black wig. It was a thin, intelligent face, with a spark of humor in the dark eyes. The soldier warmed to the atmosphere of genuine kindliness surrounding the pastor. "Now here is a friend," he told himself.

It was the more startling, therefore, when he took the hand of Merson's tall, blond nephew, to be subjected to an intense, hostile stare. Armand's breeding rescued him, and he did not return rudeness for rudeness. Perhaps, he speculated, this Mathieu had been surprised by a resemblance to someone else, though in truth, he could not have liked the person much, if so. The deacon was a colorless, impassive man about the pastor's size, but more wizened.

Still murmuring pleasantries, the gentlemen replaced their hats and everyone was seated. Now and again the black-clad nephew stole glances at Armand. His mouth was tight and censorious as he cataloged each gilt button and red ribbon on the soldier's uniform. Armand noted the schoolmaster was of a size with himself, with a boldly handsome profile and a lighter complexion. "Probably a Norman father or mother," thought Armand. "That long blond hair is his own, I'll wager, and he's not a little proud of it."

It was not until Armand saw that Mathieu was also covertly observing Madeleine Cortot that he began to understand. As Madeleine did not notice, or affected not to, that the newcomer was fishing for her eye, Mathieu's expression became increasingly glum.

"Aha!" thought Armand, now a little amused. "So that's why he scowls. One suspects me as a serpent in his little Eden!"

"Yes," Cortot was continuing, "Monsieur Gandon's father remained with the army after I left the service to go into the controller's office, back in the days when Colbert protected us of the Religion. But as I was saying, the last time the Gandons came through here was on their way to the Catalonian campaign. Now let's see, that would be in 1674. They were attached to Marshal Schomberg's staff. You are named for the Marshal, are you not?" He looked expectantly at Armand.

"Yes, I am," replied the soldier. "My father was wounded before Belleville and died the next year. The Marshal was kind enough to arrange a lieutenancy for me for the love he bore my father. I have been with the Regiment of Maine ever since."

"Ah, but Armand is no mere lieutenant these days!" Cortot seemed as pleased as if he were boasting of his own son. "In an action in the Palatinate, he saved his regiment, singlehanded, mark you, with guns and standards when they were ambushed, and he was men-

12

tioned in dispatches. He is now a major and stops with us tonight on his way from his estate in Languedoc to the Court at Versailles!"

The young officer came as near blushing as was possible for one of his weathered complexion. He fairly stammered his disclaimers.

"Monsieur Cortot is too kind, I protest! I've been so fortunate as to enjoy the interest of the Duc de Lauzières, who is colonel of my regiment. It's at his request I am to visit him on my way north."

The pastor maintained his equanimity, but the deacon and Mathieu looked shocked. Versailles was the focal point of sin and extravagance of the nation as well as the fount of Romish persecutions. To a provincial Huguenot of good morals and conventional viewpoint, Gandon's statement was like announcing his intention of going for a swim in the town sewer.

Mathieu Bertrand's expression was wonderful to behold. First distress flitted across his face, to be replaced by something approaching relief, for no proper girl would be interested in such an obvious backslider. But Papa Cortot was beaming and insensitive. Madeleine's own expression was of pleased politeness. Mathieu's face darkened again. Was not the heart of woman notoriously frail where fripperies were concerned? And here were a gold-trimmed hat, a red tassel, and much more.

More aware than Cortot of some of these reactions, Armand wished the subject might be changed. "If I had just requisitioned the fellow's horse, his sour looks would be more understandable," he thought to himself. "I must ignore him." Mademoiselle Cortot was more pleasant to look at anyway, so he addressed himself to that pleasant duty. So agreeable, in fact, he lost track of the conversation.

A cry of consternation jerked him back.

"What are you saying, pastor?" cried Cortot, half rising from his chair. His hat fell off, and his bald dome glowed pinkly in the firelight. He retrieved his hat with a shaking hand.

"You anticipate me, Brother Cortot," said the minister sadly. "Yes, the subdelegate has waited upon me within this hour and told me our temple is to be torn down within three days, and at our expense."

Madame Cortot screamed faintly and dropped her embroidery. The twins shrank closer to her and Louise buried her face in her mother's skirt. For once, Alexandre looked solemn. Madeleine stared with slightly parted lips. A long moment of silence followed. The fire sputtered fitfully. The room seemed suddenly darker and colder.

13

The pastor spoke again, quietly and slowly:

"We cannot say this visitation is unexpected. The Lord has been most gracious to His people in this place and has stayed the hand of the persecutor, unworthy though we be to claim such mercies. Now He would try us also."

"But what's their pretext?" asked Cortot.

"They say we allowed a relapsed New Convert to attend the last Communion service. You recall the lackey Petitjean? The one who lost his situation when the law was passed forbidding Huguenot servants in Catholic houses?"

Cortot nodded. "Yes, I was sent by the consistory to reason with him when he became discouraged and made scandal of the Religion by his disorderly living. I'd like to know how he came by the *mereau*.* He had to have one of the tokens to gain admission to the service."

"I heard a year ago that he'd abjured and gotten his money from the conversion fund," said the deacon.

"His name *was* on the list of New Converts sent us by the bishop," admitted the pastor.

"Well, what if it was?" snorted Madame Cortot. Her needles flashed furiously. "There must have been four or five thousand people at the last Communion."

"Certainly it is not surprising the elders did not spy the fellow," said the pastor with a sigh, "if he was even there. Of course, there are 'witnesses,' but you know what that amounts to. We have no way to dispute them, so we can only hope if he was there, that he *was* in agony of soul for his apostasy, and truly contrite."

"But at what a cost!" burst out his nephew. "For six livres—the price of a pig—he sells himself, and now we lose the last church for leagues around!"

Cortot growled. "Seeking comfort for his soul? The promise of a couple of bottles did it!"

Madame Cortot was not interested in quibbles. "What do we do now?"

"Private worship in our homes is all that is left to us, my dear sister. The law is explicit. No public worship in any building save a temple." The pastor paused sadly. "It would be well if we scattered the church records and the funds among the elders and deacons, I think. They are at my home but may be confiscated at any moment.

*Receipt given to prove attendance at church.

14

The funds let us distribute to our own poor at once. The sack of *mereaux* must be hidden, too. We may never use the tokens again, but it would not do to let them fall into the wrong hands."

"One more blow," said Cortot heavily. He smote his fist in his palm. "If anyone had told me twenty years ago how we'd have to live in 1685—"

"It *is* amazing what one can become accustomed to," agreed the pastor. " 'Patient as a Huguenot' did not become a proverb for nothing."

The fire burned low, but no one seemed to notice. Pastor Merson spoke finally:

"I doubt the Edict of Nantes will last long now—what's left of it."

"Why, they wouldn't *dare!*" stormed Madame Cortot. "The king's own grandfather made it for us."

The pastor shook his head. "You give your enemies too little credit, madame. The Edict is a poor tatter, violated in spirit and in letter."

"Well, what would you expect—" Mathieu's tone was bitter—"with cardinals for chief ministers."

"We had too many ambitious nobles in the old days, I'd say," Cortot asserted. "If it hadn't been for their fools' games against the king, I doubt he'd have paid much heed to the clamor of the clergy. Cardinal Richelieu was no fanatic. He said there should be 'no discrimination among Frenchmen except in matters of loyalty'; but who, I'd like to know, have been more loyal to the crown these past fifty years than the Huguenots? True, the Cardinal took away our political rights; but when I was young that didn't seem a great matter. We kept out of politics, and we prospered."

"I agree with you, brother," replied the pastor. "Neither Richelieu nor Mazarin was a very devoted churchman; they were first of all statesmen anxious to strengthen the crown. So they ignored the fury of the clergy and protected us. Mazarin himself said, you recall, 'I have no complaint to make of the little flock; for if it feeds in bad pasture, at least it does not go astray.' "

"This loyalty—nay, servility is a better word—what has it gotten us?" Mathieu Bertrand snorted. "Two years ago they closed forty of our churches and last year a hundred. We encourage this persecution. But there are some who do right well by licking the boots that kick them." He looked carefully at a spot in the darkness about three feet above Armand's head. The latter tightened his jaw and said nothing.

"Well, at least they have not yet dared revoke the Edict entirely," said Pastor Merson. "But with every scrape we are forced into, the Romanists always gain something. Most professions and the Crown offices are closed to us now, and our seminaries are all shut down. Mathieu here must teach school, for there is no way for him to be ordained in France, and he is forbidden to study abroad. Then, we are allowed but one primary school for each congregation, no matter how many thousands of children there may be to educate. We haven't been permitted a provincial synod for two years or a general meeting of the church for twenty-six.

"Our churches are destroyed under any pettifogging pretext. Faulty titles are found for a building which has stood for a century undisturbed, or it may be within a hundred feet of a Roman church and the singing of hymns disturbs the priest at mass. We can hold funerals only at sunrise and sunset, and there must be no more than ten mourners in any funeral procession. We must not sing our psalms on the highway or at work. If we do not uncover when the Host passes, we may be fined, beaten, or jailed. No royal insignia may be displayed in our churches, and we must allow the Roman clergy to have special benches in our temples from which they may interrupt the sermons and cause commotions in the house of the Lord.

"Unless I wish to go to prison, I must not mention in my sermons 'Egyptian bondage' or 'tyranny' or even 'troublous times.' In any document we must call ourselves the 'Pretended Reformed Religion,' the P.R.R. We can't proselytize, not even among Jews or Mohammedans. Such a great matter as letting Catholic visitors kneel during our prayers got our church in Orleans closed up. And the latest is the rule that our pastors may not stay longer than three years in a place, so it appears I shall be leaving you this summer."

Isaac Cortot spoke again, addressing his remarks to Armand:

"Perhaps as a soldier you haven't been aware of all that goes on, but if a Huguenot businessman apostatizes, he's excused debts and taxes for two years. So when you try to buy stock, you can't get credit. They're afraid you'll get 'converted' and repudiate your debts. It's hopeless in a lawsuit. All your opponent has to do is cry, 'I plead against a heretic. I have to do with a man of a religion odious to the king!'" He drew his finger across his throat expressively. "But I

16

suppose we could take this and the doubling and trebling of our taxes. The worst is the billeting. It's never a pleasure to have soldiers quartered in a decent house, but since four years ago, the Reformed have had to bear most of it, knowing that if they would but abjure, it would stop."

Madame Cortot disagreed.

"No, the worst is the lowering of the age of accountability of our children from twelve to seven, so the authorities may steal them from us and raise them Catholics!"

"It is a melancholy list," sighed the pastor, "and no human help in sight."

Mathieu Bertrand had continued to eye the almost invisible figure in the chimney corner. "Our fathers fought for *their* liberties with sword in hand," he blurted. "Now if we fight at all, we fight *for* our oppressors, it seems. Are we too timid to stand for what we believe?"

It was now quite dark, for the candles had gone out unnoticed and the fire was low. Armand promised himself that he would not let this fellow provoke him to an altercation. He stared fixedly at a large black chest near him. He had noticed earlier that it was carved with scenes from the tribulations of the children of Israel, but it was too dim to make out the details now. The pastor broke the ringing silence.

"There may be more heroism in not resisting evil, Mathieu," he said quietly. "But even if we wished to resist, would it be possible?" He, too, looked toward the officer. "What think you, Monsieur Gandon?"

Armand noticed the use of "monsieur" in place of "brother," but could not be certain that it was intentional. He picked his words carefully, and spoke directly to the minister:

"I've been in the king's army for ten years now. Louvois is the minister of war and Vauban is the greatest master of siegecraft in the world. The army has scores of regiments of infantry and cavalry ready at a moment's notice. Then there are all the new guns—and everything controlled from Versailles. Gallantry counts for little today."

Cortot rose to stir the fire. As the flames leaped up, the tense faces of the group were brought into sharp relief.

"I agree with you, Armand," said Cortot. "I was a soldier once, and even in my day we could see it coming. The power of the

Crown is established now. I think when the nobility saw the king was supreme and it was hopeless to resist, they lost their interest in religion. I don't say all of them were this way, you understand, but far too many. The gentry were always lax, careless of their deportment and in Sabbath observance. And even the great Turenne left us. Now all we have left is this threadbare Edict."

"Perhaps this is God's way to make us more aware of our dependence on Him," the minister said gently. "Certainly we have no other refuge. As for those who have left us, be it Marshal Turenne or this poor Petitjean, we cannot know the heart. We should pray for their repentance and soon return."

"Maybe we should have listened to Claude Brousson two years ago," said Cortot, resuming his seat, "when the brethren in Toulouse wanted us to fast and pray publicly on an appointed day, law or no law, temple or no temple, in all meekness of course, that the king might see how many we were and pause before he went too far."

"Nay, brother," replied the pastor solemnly. "You know I opposed that scheme. Resistance simply plays into the hands of our persecutors. The clergy wish for nothing better than to convince His Majesty that we are disloyal and will make party with his enemies.

"God enjoins obedience to earthly sovereigns," he continued, "for they were ordained by Him. On this the Scriptures are very clear. All we have is at the disposal of Caesar, save for our consciences."

Madame Cortot shook a long needle at the pastor.

"But surely we can't allow the king's men to carry off all that we have worked for, the inheritance of our children, yes, even the children themselves! Are we to flee to alien lands and bring up our children among strangers—to beg their bread perhaps?"

"We are told in Matthew 10:23 that 'when they persecute you in this city, flee ye into another.'" The pastor spoke reprovingly. "But while we should count it no loss to leave all for the Lord's sake, it is also true that there are times when it is better to abide in one's place and faithfully live the truth.

"We have changed, not the Lord," he added. "We are waxen fat and increased with goods. All hate the Huguenot. He is wealthy, for he works harder and longer than his Catholic neighbor—fifty extra days a year because he does not keep saints' days. His sober living is a rebuke. He presumes to think differently in the realm of a king who wishes his subjects to conform in all things."

"Our enemies have been crying woe for ninety years," interjected his nephew. "Why do we then have so much trouble now?"

"It may be a change in the king himself," said the pastor slowly. "He has in the past laid a heavy hand on the pope and may need now to prove his orthodoxy. He has eschewed his immoral way of life and may need to show his piety by harshness toward heretics. I am sure his confessor whispers in his ear; and there's our ancient enemy, Chancellor Le Tellier, the father of Louvois; and there is much talk of this woman at court who, it is said, has secretly become his wife. She used to be the nurse of the king's children, and 'tis said she has great influence over him. And to think she was born a Protestant!" He paused. "In any case, the English philosopher Bacon spoke truth when he said that no man doeth a wrong for wrong's sake, but to gain himself profit, pleasure, or honor."

The fire had almost died again. It flickered unevenly and sent irregular shadows chasing each other vainly about the walls. Louise had gone to sleep on her mother's knee and Louis sat with heavy-lidded eyes, swaying occasionally. Madeleine was gazing abstractedly into the fire. Armand was thinking he had never seen anything quite as pretty as Madeleine's face with the firelight on it.

"The Lord's people may be approaching the climax of their tribulations," concluded the pastor. "We must be firm in our minds, ready to accept flight or the dungeon, whatever He sends, with meekness and joy that we are accounted worthy to suffer for Him."

CHAPTER 2

I

ARMAND DE GANDON awoke with a start. For an uneasy moment he had the feeling that he was in the wrong place. A quick glance around the bare, windowless cell and it all came back to him. Uneasiness changed to excitement. He was in one of the loft rooms of the Grand Commun, the vast dormitory for the royal household at Versailles. Today he was to accompany his great and good friend, the Duc de Lauzières, to the court of the *Grande Monarque*.

It was a chill morning, a reminder of departed winter. By the light of a single candle stub, his roommate was adjusting his wig before a fragment of mirror on the wall. Through the flimsy partitions a subdued rustling, like the sound of a regiment of rats, told of hundreds of menials of greater and lesser degree also preparing for another day.

Armand swung his feet out of the so-called bed and grunted with shock as they touched the freezing planks. He reached shivering for his breeches and began to dress carefully. His new clothes deserved some care, for they had cost him nearly a year's income from his poor estate down south. But then, one could not circulate in this milieu for nothing.

The breeches and the coat were of sky blue. Bunches of ribbons ornamented the shoulders and sleeves, and there were many buttons. He wore a russet *justaucorps** as long as the coat, and used as a vest. This was trimmed in silver lace. The full white shirt was gathered at the wrists. The coat was to be worn open, the vest buttoned. A lawn cravat tied by a ribbon was at his throat, and the opening of the shirt was concealed by a *jabot*** of lace. The shoes, not particularly comfortable, were of black leather with red heels and linings.

*A close coat.
**Frill.

Armand thought the heel taller and narrower than was safe, but those Parisian merchants cowed one so that one lacked the temerity to suggest a more substantial model. The big silver bows on the shoes and the dandyish stiffening and flaring of the skirt of the coat made him feel a bit ridiculous also. He had to remind himself that here he was a courtier, not a soldier. On a rickety chair nearby lay a fine black beaver hat, the brim turned up at the sides, garnished with silver lace and with an ostrich plume lying within the brim. Add to all this yellow stockings, a curly black wig (he simply could not afford a light-colored one), a dress sword with a fringed knot, and a silver-headed cane, and he would be ready to face the polite world.

The other young man was now dressed and had stepped to the door.

"At the hotel," he said, and jerked a thumb over his shoulder. Armand nodded.

Before putting on his neckcloth and coat, Armand stepped over to the night stand by the other cot. With a thoughtful forefinger he tested the water in the basin. The Huguenot fires had been burning rather low in him in recent days. As he had ridden north from Saint Martin two weeks earlier, the somber prospects of his Protestant friends had weighed much on his mind. He even speculated a little uneasily about the dangers of his own course. Would his head be turned by the vanities of the great city and the preferment of a duke?

"Just a country bumpkin come to town," he said to himself as he dashed the stinging water on his face. But sophisticates knew that washing with water was dangerous. It was safer, if one *must* wash, to use watered wine, as did the king. There were so many things to learn. He sighed. He had never had to concern himself with these extreme points of decorum, but here one never addressed anyone simply as "monsieur." That was very bourgeois. In the Versailles chateau itself, he must remember, one never knocked. One scratched on doors with the nail of a little finger. In the houses of the town one never scratched, but knocked. Of course, at a lady's door one used the knocker once—no more. And if he had it straight, it was the small end of the boiled egg one must cut, not the large end. Truly the opportunities to show oneself to disadvantage were endless.

As he straightened up to adjust his cravat, he bumped his head on a beam of the sloping ceiling. For one of his height, the ceilings on these cubicles were not adequate at all. The ducal party had reached Versailles the previous evening, and the duke had put up at a friend's house. But even an influential person could not provide for most of his dependents, and some had to double up around the corner in one of the thousand rooms of the Grand Commun. Armand steadied his new wig, which was a trifle longer than he was accustomed to, and put on his hat. Blowing out the candle, he stepped into the fourth-floor hallway, foul with odors of bad cooking and unwashed humanity.

Most of the tide that flowed out of the front doors of the Grand Commun was in the livery of one of the seven services of the royal household, or of the seven services of the queen, the dauphin, or the dauphine. But some were gentlemen like Armand who needed quarters for the night and were now hurrying to the ceremonial rising of their patrons, who in their turn would be expected to assist at the *levée** of His Majesty at eight.

"Big fleas have little fleas," thought Armand, "and behold the newest of the little ones." He rounded the corner of the Grand Commun, passed behind the red secretariat building and on to the Place d'Armes. A brisk walk of several hundred yards on to the Avenue de Paris brought him to the duke's quarters. It was just six, and the sun was almost up.

Getting up in the morning was a high point of the day when a personage was concerned. When the *levée* was conducted in a small chamber, such as that where the duke had spent the night, it was very like a booth at the Palais Royal. The great man was out of bed now (Armand had arrived a minute late) and seated near his dressing table, hemmed in by a thick cloud of servants and sycophants. A fire smoldered in the grate, and the air was close enough to cut with a knife. His Grace, in a striped silk dressing gown, sipped tea for his digestion's sake, complained of his rheumatics in a high nasal voice, and held court for his retainers simultaneously. His bald head protruded from the neckcloth used to keep the unguents from soiling the dressing gown, and his deep black eyes swung this way and that as he followed the talk. While his valet applied the cosmetics to his wizened face and another servant held up wigs for his choice, pretty gentlemen and near-gentlemen scraped in as close as they could, begging favors, flattering and fawning. Had his gouty

*Arising.

22

leg not been out in front of him on a footstool, they would have cut the duke off from his fire and completely submerged him.

Armand's tardy arrival caused a mild sensation. Usually it was a task to fight one's way to the center where one could gaze respectfully upon the glistening cranium of the eminent man, but Armand was new, obviously in high favor, and therefore heartily disliked by everyone who gravitated around this ducal sun. His competitors hoped to see some sign of displeasure, and a frown for Armand would have cheered them greatly. They allowed him to work his way through rather easily and make his reverences, sweeping the floor with his hat, his hand touching the planks.

The duke appeared to note nothing amiss. His face crinkled in a pleased grin, and he graciously allowed the newcomer to kiss his bony hand.

His Grace then dropped a bombshell. He casually mentioned that Monsieur de Gandon would accompany him to His Majesty's own *levée* that morning, that he might pay homage to the sovereign in person. The retinue was breathless with envy, and for a moment Armand himself could not speak. Only the duke's high favor with the king would make it thinkable to introduce such an insignificant person into such august surroundings. As the retinue went out of the hotel into the blessed crispness of the spring morning, it would have been a far duller person than Armand de Gandon not to realize that he was deeply unpopular with everyone but the old duke himself.

Bearers carried the duke's blue lacquered sedan chair down the avenue, past the royal stables, through the first gate, across the cobbles of the Place d'Armes. The swarm of clients accompanied him afoot until they reached the great gilded portals embellished with the blue and gilt arms of France. Stone sentry boxes flanked the main gate, and on top of them were marble groups representing victories over Austria and Spain. They gleamed pinkly in the morning sun. Already the fencing was taking on a golden glow, and the impressionable visitor was struck with the unspeakable wealth and power of France—the center of the world.

At this point sedan chairs were available for six sous, in which one might ride in style across the court of the Chateau to a vestibule of the palace. No carriages ever penetrated there except those of royalty. Armand would have preferred the short walk but feared to embarrass the duke by some little *gaucherie*,* so he hired a chair and two blue-coated bearers to take him to the plain doorway of the chateau.

On Armand's arm, the duke proceeded through hallways and corridors of the new palace, followed by all the pack. Using his cane as a pointer, the duke kept up a constant stream of comment on the chambers through which they passed. He pointed out the abilities or failures of the artists responsible for their embellishment. He mentioned who had been camping in each room, for in that over-crowded place it was a mark of great distinction to sleep in one of the public rooms, even though one could hardly be abed until early in the morning and must needs arise very soon thereafter. Only the greatest grandees could win an airless cubicle on an upper floor of the chateau. The swarms of unfamiliar faces left Armand in a sort of stupor—he could assimilate only so much in so short a time. He did notice that they met no women, for the women's *levées* were not for another hour yet.

After a number of turns, they reached a series of anterooms and some of the retinue dropped off, unable to approach farther toward the royal sleeping chamber. They would wait the reemergence of the duke and the gentlemen, for that was after all the best hope of swarms of freeloaders, or *cherche-midis*—a meal at noon and a bed for the night.

The duke, Armand, and the other gentry entered the dimly lit Chambre of the Oeil-de-Boeuf. Glancing about cautiously, Armand could see why the room had the name, for up on the right wall near the ceiling was a large eye-shaped window of colored glass which was beginning to shed a soft radiance on the throng below. One's eye was drawn up past the gilt stucco ornamentation on the cornices to the vaulted white ceiling. Richly carved and gilded doors led on the one hand to the king's bedchamber and on the other to the Grand Gallery.

Pressed in the room were the great of France, clothed in every hue of the rainbow, in every expensive fabric procurable by the tailors of the world's fashion center. Jeweled rings, buttons, and sword hilts added flashing points of light to the symphony of colored silks and satins.

Though not extraordinarily sensitive or timid, Armand swallowed with sudden apprehension. He was overcome by a feeling of insig-

*Awkwardness.

nificance and presumption at trespassing here. All about him were peers, generals, and marshals, the holders of the most ancient and exalted titles in the land, arrogant men, some of whom could trace their lineage back centuries before the king's own House of Bourbon had come down out of the southern mountains. Yet it would be unthinkable for them not to be present at the arising of the monarch.

In all France the gentle dew of favors and advancement came from this one source. Since but one sun shone, for a noble not to strive to place himself under those beneficent rays was to resign himself to outer darkness. Even the greatest nobles wore themselves out in this constant attendance and the deadly rivalry it entailed. How dull, how profitless was life on one's estates! Even the lesser nobility were expected to show themselves. Not to be near, not to be seen by the king on every possible occasion every day, could lead to the most crushing and final of rejections, "I never see him."

Few seemed to be running that risk this morning, thought Armand, and he dazedly supported the duke as he circulated through the throng exchanging civilities with friends and enemies.

As eight o'clock approached, the tension in the room rose. The buzz of conversation took on a higher pitch. Even now the royal watchmaker was in the sleeping chamber to wind the royal watch, the wigmaker from the wig cabinet next door to leave a selection of wigs with which to start the day, and the royal faggot bearers to build a royal fire—not perhaps an important matter to a king who always slept with covers at hip level, winter and summer. These formalities were known to all the world, and it was said that one had but to look at his watch in any part of France to know what Louis XIV was doing at that moment.

Emotion now ran even higher. The king was being informed that it was eight o'clock, he being presumed to have slept through the preliminaries. The crowd in the anteroom swayed gently like tall grass in a light breeze. The greatest dignitaries gathered close to the door, proud in the exclusive privilege of the *grande entrée*. Within, the First Physician and the First Surgeon waited on the king to change his shirt and to give him his rubdown. At a quarter past the hour, the door was flung open and the Grand Chamberlain was admitted with a select group. With the *grande entrée* went the duke. Armand remained behind in the press of lesser mortals who lacked birth, function, or favor.

25

A few moments later, the remainder of the court nobility were permitted in, after giving their names to the doorkeeper. As they entered the stuffy room, the king was just putting on his breeches, a feat he performed with the dexterity and grace of one who had been doing it in public for decades. When the time came for the shirt, it was handed by the First Valet to the senior person present, who happened to be the Duc de Lauzières. Before the envious and awe-stricken eyes of his fellow peers, the old man then handed the shirt to the king.

As he stood behind the carved and gilded balustrade, Armand was prey to powerful emotions. That he should be this close to his king! Once before he had seen the monarch. It had been at a review, and he had thrilled with pride as the regiment had marched past while the king and his courtiers stood watching on a little mound. Armand had marched with drawn sword at the salute, just behind the colors and in front of the ranks. He had felt rather than seen the sovereign on that occasion, for the colonel-duke had instructed his men to slightly avert their gaze from the Sun King, as if his glory hurt their eyes. (The duke was clever at such tactful touches, somewhat better in fact than he was on the battlefield.) Now, with swimming head, Armand stood not fifteen feet from the greatest king on earth, the embodiment of France!

As he gaped in solemn pride, the pageant continued with each of the players skillfully performing his accustomed role, but none so well versed in the tableau as the king himself. Every one of his sixty-five inches added to the effect of superb dignity and gracious-ness. The nobility, traditional competitors of the Crown, were now completely his. They had no power, but now prized their nearness to the throne instead—the right to hold the royal shirt, to be the first to greet majesty in the morning, craving the casual, trivial word which would elevate them among their peers, repair their fortunes, or gain them additional time with their creditors.

It was not His Majesty's day to shave, nor to wash his face and hands. The king did mention quite forcefully that Lent was approach-ing, and he would take it very ill if he heard that anyone about the Court should eat meat on those sacred days—unless they were very old or had a doctor's certificate.

When he had finished dressing, the conversation turned as usual to hunting. This gave Armand an opportunity to study the magnificences of the sleeping chamber—the white-and-gold doors, the fire-places of bluish marble at each end, and the huge mirrors with sculptured and gilded frames. The cornices were masses of gilding, too, with the arms of France and the cipher of the monarch worked into the scheme. The west wall was of crimson velvet. Beneath a gilded pavilion, on an estrade, stood the king's bed. At each corner of the canopy sprouted white plumes. Out the windows, beyond the courtyard, one could see the sunlit Avenue de Paris.

The king finished his cup of hippocras* and proceeded to prayers. As he knelt on the *prie-dieu*** by his bed, the ecclesiastics present plumped to their knees also, but the laity remained standing with heads bared. Then the monarch rose, saluted the assemblage courteously, and withdrew to an inner chamber, his particular favorites flowing after him like a loose-jointed tail. The ordinary sort drifted out of the chamber to await nine o'clock mass in the temporary chapel.

As his mind began to recover a little, Armand found his Huguenot conscience still alive, if feeble. He knew he was expected to join the duke for mass. But concentrated thinking resulted happily, and he consoled himself with a precedent: had not Naaman held the arm of the king of Syria in the temple of Rimmon?

II

THIS was Thursday, so the king granted private audiences. (He customarily met his council three mornings a week, and his confessor on Fridays.) Armand was beginning to discover that a courtier's duties required a lot of standing. He tried to shift his weight from one foot to another as unobtrusively as possible. Either the marble flooring was marvelously hard or his high heels were betraying him. Sitting was unthinkable for the common herd, but they remained outside the royal chambers gossiping, criticizing, talking endlessly about hunting, fashions, and the pettiest of matters, eyeing with practiced calculation all who entered or left the Presence, estimating to a hair's breadth the standing of favorites, and scenting to a marvelous nicety any shift in the wind.

Armand had not eaten, and his head was beginning to ache as

*Spiced wine.
**Kneeling desk for use at prayer.

well as his feet. How like a disorderly chicken coop, he thought, as they peck away at each other. He had been shocked in the chapel, too. He could remember the Huguenot services of his boyhood, and except for a couple of times when two nobles had quarreled over precedence in the pews, the dignity and decorum had been noteworthy. Here at Versailles the worshipers (to use the term loosely) came to be seen by the king, who did not appear to care if they chatted, flirted, or told indecent stories throughout the service.

His train of thought was interrupted every so often by ornate exchanges with passing courtiers. Armand felt himself coloring like a girl. "At Saint Martin," he thought bitterly, shifting his weight once more, "I pass for a man of the world, a model of elegance and polish—yes, am even suspected of turning the heads of virtuous maidens; here, without doubt, I have the standing of a dancing bear at a country fair. Not that I haven't met aristocratic snobs in plenty in the army. But here, to succeed one must be hard as glass and know when to be silent, when to be bold, when to scrape invisibly along the wall, and when to drop a friend. Also, one must cultivate an eye that misses nothing, and an instinct for knowing what the king is going to do and how to be seen by him when he does it. I would I were out of this," he was saying to himself, when suddenly everything changed.

A gorgeous gentleman usher in pink silks and a powdered wig announced the audience of the Duc de Lauzières. Before he realized it, Armand found himself entering the king's presence with the duke on his arm.

Louis XIV sat in a high-backed chair by a large table piled with papers. He had good legs, and they were crossed now to show them to best advantage. He greeted the pair in fatherly fashion. The king was half a head shorter, but the calm gaze of the gray-green eyes, the undeniable majesty of his demeanor, made one forget physical size, the protruding lip, and the pockmarks. Here was a king who had performed his role so long that he was no longer conscious of playacting when he claimed to be God's lieutenant on earth.

Elegant as His Majesty appeared, his dress was plainer than that of most of the courtiers. The king wore his favorite brown. The blue ribbon of the Order of the Holy Ghost crossed his embroidered long vest. He wore no jewels save for stones in his garters and shoe buckles, but his peruke was enormous.

28

The duke presented the young soldier and dwelt on the exploit of six years earlier, which he pretended the king would recall, but he tactfully refrained from any mention of the major's Huguenot background. The king responded most graciously and seemed pleased by Armand's confusion—a reaction he rather liked in those who met their king for the first time.

Before he realized it, Armand found himself discussing the current controversy over whether pikes should still be carried in the infantry.

"Louvois is decidedly for keeping pikemen in addition to musketeers," observed the king.

"Louvois is a—" The major colored crimson and wished he might sink between the tiles. The king smiled.

"There are times when I am inclined to agree with you, though he is one of my most capable servants. But pray proceed."

"Forgive me, Your Majesty. What I should have said was that the first thing a pikeman does on any battlefield is to throw his pike away and procure himself a musket. If all our infantry were expert in musketry, we should have no need for pikes. I fear the war minister does not have the field experience to see it as lower officers do." The king seemed interested, and Armand's confidence began to return. The audience concluded with a discussion of uniforms.

"If all ranks might wear uniforms, your majesty would be better served, for it would eliminate the deserter and the *passe volant**almost at a blow, and would prevent some grievous errors in battle."

The king objected to the cost, and before he knew it, the major was once again arguing with the king. The latter seemed to enjoy it, and took the difference of opinion in good humor since it was done with proper submissiveness.

"What a grasp of detail! What a kindly manner!" thought Armand, much impressed. "He's not the ogre we Huguenots fear, yet how can such a king be so harsh to our people? If they could but get to him—"

"You have served us well," the king was saying, "and your career promises to be a brilliant one. You are fortunate in the friendship of the duke."

He inclined his head to terminate the audience.

*A civilian temporarily drafted so that an officer could display a larger number of soldiers than he actually commanded, and fraudulently claim additional money from the king for their support.

"I live but to serve Your Majesty," murmured Armand. He and the duke backed from the king's presence.

As they emerged into the anterooms, Armand noted a change in the atmosphere. "Here is someone on the way up!" whispered the perspicacious. As he followed the duke through the press, it seemed that lords and ladies alike wished to be friends. It was really rather amusing what a quarter of an hour could do, he thought wryly.

III

AT DUSK Armand stood under the chestnuts in the Versailles gardens with his hands clasped behind. He listened with one ear only as the duke, seated on a stone bench, was describing the building up of the chateau from the neglected hunting lodge of Louis XIII to its present magnificence. They were on a side path near the Allée d'Été. Close by, the goddess Flora lounged in a basin with winged cupids. A line of silent statues sloped gently down to a greater basin where Apollo sat enthroned in a four-horse chariot. Beyond lay the Grand Canal, the fading light gleaming redly on its tranquil surface. Few of the 1,400 jets were on, for water was still a problem on this arid plain, and the works to bring the River Eure over to the king's gardens were not yet completed. The cinder paths were hard on dress shoes, and it was with gratitude that one found benches among the groves.

The duke was making some unflattering suppositions about the contractors and guessing at total construction costs, but Armand was reliving the high points of the day. He had been impressed, for example, by the king's *diner en public,** and wondered, with the circuitous route the food had to travel from another building, and the tasting of all dishes, whether the king had ever enjoyed a hot meal.

He also recalled the review of the French and Swiss Guards in the courtyard of the chateau, right below the royal bedchamber. He especially envied the Life Guards in scarlet and blue accompanied by trumpeters and preceded by their Negro cymbal player dressed in splendor like a Turkish sultan. These were elite corps where even the common soldiers were gentle born. After watching their evolutions, he regretfully promised himself that here was something he would have to work on when he returned to the regiment.

*Dinner eaten in public.

But the duke was still gossiping. He talked so much that he did not seem to mind if his listeners were not always with him.

"Never stand when you can sit, my boy!" he cackled happily. "You have strong young shanks now, but they'll wear out fast on these marble floors. Sit down, sit down!" Armand sat.

The light was failing rapidly. It was too dark to see the snuff discolorations on the duke's suit of plum satin. His blue silk ribbon of the Holy Ghost appeared white now in the dimness. The air was mild, for the afternoon had warmed considerably. The scent of the flowers was heavy; the king liked the more potent varieties and he liked them renewed frequently.

"How do you find Versailles now?" inquired the old man, squinting up intently at the young officer.

"It is somewhat overwhelming to one used to the camp or the country, my lord. There is so much to learn, but it is a great privilege to be here and to see the magnificence all the world talks of."

"True, but I didn't bring you out here to listen to birds or to admire statuary."

Armand turned to look at him, a little surprised.

"I've had my eye on you for a long time, major; in fact, ever since that occasion six years ago when you proved yourself in the field," asserted the duke, and Armand dropped his eyes modestly. "I have felt that you have justified your promotions many times over. I have always been satisfied that I recommended them."

He stabbed with his cane in the general direction of the chateau.

"Now, the king, as you know, is raising twenty-seven new regiments of infantry. (Why just now, with the world at peace, I don't know. But one is permitted to guess.)" He winked in conspiratorial fashion, which screwed his seamed face into a thousand wrinkles. He leaned forward and dropped his voice, but it rasped enough to cut through the tinkling of the waters. "For the time, it pleases me to remain as colonel of my own regiment, but I intend to arrange for you the colonelcy of one of the new regiments—if you think you would be interested. The king will agree, I've little doubt, though the commission might take a little time to complete."

Armand did not hear the concluding words. His mind reeled. He was glad to be sitting down. A regiment for the taking? He could not speak. The duke watched him quizzically, apparently enjoying the effect of his own words. For a chance like this, hundreds of the nobility pawned their own and their relations' assets and flocked to court. Few were ever so fortunate. Why, just that morning Armand overheard some talk that the Marquis de Soyecourt had paid 42,000 livres for the Vermandois regiment. A really good regiment, like one of the Swiss, might run up to 60,000. Armand would not earn that much in his lifetime from his estate and officer's pay put together! Stammering his gratitude, he protested his unworthiness.

"Nonsense!" snapped the duke. "I know what I'm doing. We can talk more of that later, but I thought you should know what's in the wind. If you are concerned about my kin, pray calm yourself. Those ghouls can hardly wait till I'm dumped in a grave, but we Robillarts are a tough lot. At seventy-one, I'm a mere boy! I'll have the laugh on them yet—in more ways than they suspect." He winked at the dumbfounded Armand. "A colonelcy for one of them? Servile curs and sneak thieves! They have the martial virtues of weevils in a biscuit! A hundred years ago, it would have been my pleasure to hang the lot of them, but these are degenerate times and *seigneurs*** no longer enjoy their rightful powers."

"But sir, you are too kind—"

"What were you going to say? Don't bother. I do not appreciate being argued with."

Armand's mouth closed helplessly.

"Would you be more interested if you had a little pocket money, to live in proper style?" the duke asked.

The young major thought rather dazedly of the weary years behind and the many more he had expected as a career officer on four *louis d'or*** a month. He had always assumed that for the rest of his life he would do the work while titled loafers with purchased commissions took the credit and the promotions. He remembered the bitter snubs and insults, how he had resented their arrogance, their ignorance, their caracoling horses, their wines, silver, and fine clothes. He thought of the young officers who bankrupted themselves and turned thief, trying to live up to that extravagance. He himself had long ago turned his back on competitive magnificence, swallowing his pride, or rather making it a matter of pride to live on his pay. And, of course, for such parsimony, one suffered more grievous ridicule. Well, all of that could be left behind now.

*Feudal lords.
**A gold coin.

32

"My lord, what *can* I say? It's like a fairy tale!"

"Well then, colonel," said the duke, reading his answer in the younger man's rapt face, "let's not talk here longer. It's almost time for the *appartement*.*" He heaved himself stiffly to his feet and took Armand's arm. "Since the good old days of the divine Athenais, matters run more soberly around the Court—though I think there will be enough of interest to give you an enjoyable evening. Fie on that gloomy Madame Maintenon! 'Tis she who has scared our poor king so badly about his soul that if this keeps up, Versailles will turn into a convent, I fear."

The two men strolled slowly back toward the terrace of the chateau.

"His Majesty was pleased with you this morning, and we would do well to keep him in that opinion. Your *gaffe*** on Louvois was sheer genius. The great minister is indispensable to good King Louis, but he's hard to get along with—a surly churl, and lately he has ruffled the royal temper. An experienced courtier could not have improved upon your ingenuous blurt—beautifully timed, and it appeared quite sincere." The duke laughed at Armand's discomfiture.

"Oh, I know you didn't intend it. That's what made it so successful! Now, one of the ways we keep our royal master well-disposed toward us is to be present at the *appartements*. He has the rare gift of walking in on these affairs and being able to tell at a glance who is not there. I would much rather be in Paris this evening, but our gracious lord does not care much for his capital city, and there would be inquiries about those who presumed to steal away for entertainment elsewhere. In the circumstances, I think I shall remain here, bored rigid probably, but visible."

IV

THE thin and graceful strains of Lulli's orchestra floated through the tall windows of the chateau as the soldier and the duke mounted the broad terrace. Since the old man was short of breath, they paused a moment. It was dark now and the stronger stars had appeared. Fountains played and the waters sparkled in the

*Entertainment held in the Court.
**Blundering remark.

light from the windows. Couples strolled about on the terrace. Snatches of laughter mingled with the music. Reflected light made pastel shades on the palace walls. A jewel on someone's costume sparkled occasionally. The scented evening was pure enchantment.

This dream chateau was no more splendid than possibilities opening before him, thought Armand. A courtier, in high favor, with a powerful patron—where might it not end? A title? A marshal's baton? What did the duke mean? He had no son now—he'd been killed in Germany in the battle which had won Armand his chance. His thoughts were already intoxicating enough.

He glanced up at the shimmering stars, and a sudden twinge of guilt troubled him. What would this do to his religion? He had never made much of it before, to be sure. As a soldier he'd managed a certain suppleness of conscience. Why could he not manage just as well at court, too? No one had asked him to apostatize, had he?

The duke turned in from the terrace toward the Salon of Venus and the Little Gallery. A portly bishop, with the jowly distinction of a Roman emperor, approached the pair at the foot of the Ambassador's Staircase. After introductions, the duke transferred his grasp to the churchman's sleeve.

"Go enjoy yourself, my boy," he said airily. "His Grandeur and I have a little score to settle, a matter of a thousand louis I took from him at *picquet** last summer. He thinks he can do something about it now, and it is only civil that I give him the opportunity." He saluted Armand with his walking stick. "Win or lose, the curse will be off the evening." He laughed raspingly, and he and the bishop went off to their game.

Armand contented himself for a time by standing and admiring the staircase. Then he gazed up at the marble vault soaring to the roof of the chateau, and at the superb landing with the fountain playing in its niche and the white bust of the king in its niche above. On each side rose more steps from the landing. Over the balustrades the Court could look down at mere foreigners ascending the lower flight to make their submission to the Sun King awaiting them on the landing. Tapestries of the king's victories hung on the walls. The ceiling was aswarm with personified arts, sciences, and virtues.

As he drifted through the crowded apartments, Armand felt almost suffocated by the magnificence about him. The Salon of Venus was

*A card game.

in marble mosaic. The goddess ruled the ceiling. She was painted crowned by the Graces and she had the unlikely company of Augustus, Nebuchadnezzar, Alexander, and Cyrus. The draperies and the furniture were splendid in green and gold. Liveried servants piled up pyramids of fruits, flowers, and confections on silver tables. Eight-branched candlesticks of cut glass and silver illuminated the scene.

Armand passed through the stunning Salon of Diana, in its crimson-and-gold decor, to the ballroom, the Salon of Mars, with a marble tribune over to the left for the musicians. The god of battles rode his wolf car across the ceiling escorted by Caesar, Cyrus, Marcus Aurelius, and Constantine. Two huge silver-and-glass chandeliers swung overhead. Silver also gleamed in the tables set between the windows, in flower baskets, candlesticks, and punchbowls. The draperies were in green velvet with gold fringes.

Tonight the card players had the chamber. Blue-liveried footmen dispensed counters and kept the score. The din was fearful. Angry and excited voices overtopped the normal roar of conversation. Here was one of the few places a courtier was entitled to sit down, but from an excess of scruples and a shortage of cash, Armand resisted the temptation. He spotted the duke and the bishop hard at play. The latter was losing again. His face was red and perspiring and his language sufficient to give respectful pause even to an infantry major.

Armand passed through two more gorgeous chambers, then through a large arch which led into the noblest spectacle of all, the Grand Gallery.

The flames of four thousand candles were reflected in nineteen tall mirrors set between the windows. The hall swept off 240 feet into the distance. Four years of labor by Lebrun had been dedicated to the glory of the *Grande Monarque* on the ceiling alone. Because of its height, the thirty allegories of the young Louis XIV and his victories were only dimly visible, observed by the impressionable soldier through a golden haze of equal parts candle smoke and splendor.

Armand stood rooted to the spot. In the subdued light it was a hall of luminous shadows, of things half glimpsed, fabrics and marbles softly blended. The Savonnierie carpets underfoot were sensed rather than seen. There was the impression of gleaming silver, not a clear picture of tables, orange tubs, and chandeliers. Whether it was crystal lusters, the white damask curtains with the royal cipher in gold, or green-and-gold draperies, he could not pick any one thing out. Around him milled hundreds of courtiers, the opulence of their dress softened by the effect of the candlelight on iridescent fabrics and metallic lace. Pale faces and white shoulders glowed in unwonted perfection. His ears were filled with the murmur of hundreds of voices, the rustling of satins, and snatches of distant music. He stood speechless with pride and wonder, viewing this abode of demigods.

Progressing slowly through the throng came the center of all the adoration. As he made his stately way, Louis XIV smiled graciously at this one, inclined an ear politely to the appeal of that one, leaving ripples of joy or disappointment in his wake. But he never refused or agreed on the spot. "I will see," he would murmur in his majestic but gentlemanly way. The captain of the guard pressed behind him, always at the king's back, his eyes roving restlessly to and fro.

Unfashionably bronzed, tall and handsome as he was, Armand did not escape notice. The bashful major was taken over by a determined blonde in crimson satin. Her hair was well powdered and she wore her black beauty patches in the style called "kisses." She played her wide blue eyes on him like a battery, but neither her natural nor artificial charms breached his reserve.

She had added six inches to her slight stature by her high-wired *fontange*,* fluttering with ribbons and beautified with pleated ruffles, but the top of it came scarcely to his eyes. She chattered constantly and kept him busy fighting his way in and out of the Salon of Venus to fetch her sweetmeats and glazed fruits from the huge mounds on the sideboards, and in between he made trips for her to the punchbowl. But she only secured his full attention once, and that was when he stepped on her train. For the rest of it, for his taste, she was oversupplied with conversation and pockmarks.

"My dear hopeful Countess Whatever-your-name-is," he said to himself as he returned once more from the refreshment tables, "on my pay I couldn't keep you in lace." Then he remembered that his fortune was in flood and began to realize at least one of the problems fortune might bring.

The blonde would have been even more discouraged had she realized that her taciturn target was comparing her with a tall brunette who had never been near Versailles. If Madeleine were only here, he mused, listening absently to the rattle of his companion. What would she think of this wonderful place? And of his good luck? How would

*A fancy headdress.

she look in a court gown, with a high *fontange* and a trailing *manteau**? That magnificent complexion of hers—how it would be set off by candlelight in the Hall of Mirrors! She would look a veritable queen, he told himself. How far would she surpass the late real queen of France—sallow, dumpy, snag-toothed Maria Theresa!

Supper was at ten, and there Armand lost the blonde, baffled but game, ready to try again tomorrow. The king put away another huge meal, eating silently *au grande couvert,*** under the devoted eyes of the court. Feeling a little peaked, he ate only three bowls of soup, a whole pheasant and a whole partridge, some mutton with garlic, a slice of ham, a salad, some fruit, hard-boiled eggs, and pastry.

Louis then adjourned to his bedroom where, leaning against the balustrade before his bed, he received the curtsies of the ladies. Then he bowed, gave the password and countersign to the captain of the guard, and retired to his private chamber to be with his family. The doors were left open, and the courtiers assembling for the *coucher*† stood in the dogs' room and watched the king and his brother seated in armchairs, the ladies on taborets, and the dauphin standing.

After a long hour of this, during which Armand almost went to sleep erect, he joined the courtiers massed expectantly in the bedchamber for the *grande coucher.*

The king said his prayers under scores of eyes, and selected a distinguished courtier for the honor of taking the candlestick from the first *valet de chambre.*†† When His Majesty finished undressing, he dismissed the Court with another bow. With the majority, Armand now left the room and waited in the Oeil-de-Boeuf for the grandees who had the honor of the *petit coucher.*

Eventually the sovereign was under the coverlet and alone, except for his valet (who would sleep beyond the balustrade on a camp bed) and a midnight snack left for him on a night table—a matter of three loaves, two bottles of wine, water, and three cold dishes.

Armand did not remember much about the *coucher* of the duke. By this time he was more dead than alive, but they got the old man into bed somehow and the soldier limped back to the Grand Commun, his mind still whirling with the tremendous events of the day. His feet were on fire, his eyes gritty.

*Coat.
**Publicly and ceremoniously.
†Retirement.
††Room servant.

At 1:30 in the morning he reached the top of the creaking stairs and opened the door of his garret. The room was airless and stifling; the pallet hard as the wooden trestle supporting it. He would have to be up again at six, but he was too tired and happy to care. He fell asleep almost instantly.

V

WHEN the lawyers at Versailles drew up the edict banning Huguenot services, they overlooked the picnic. The congregation of the former church at Saint Martin gathered around their pastor in the corner of a meadow about a mile from town while he asked the Lord's blessing on their picnic lunch. Certainly no one could object to that. It was true, if any wished to quibble, that the prayer was suspiciously like a sermon in tone and length.

When Pastor Merson had finished, the group began to break up into smaller ones. The older men gathered in knots to talk and the married women and unattached girls started to prepare the food.

"I hope the Lord is not angered by our manner of worship," said one elderly man with drooping antique mustaches.

"I'm not especially worried about the Lord," said Cortot, shading his eyes with his hand as he searched the edges of the meadow. "I'm certain He understands our predicament well enough, but I don't doubt those rascals over yonder beyond the fence are keeping good watch over us."

"I hope watching makes them good and hungry," said a plump young woman spitefully.

"Clouds!" exclaimed the pastor, glancing up. "Just a few so far. I hope it doesn't rain. The whole day free from our vexations would do us all good."

"Then you might have mentioned it in your prayer," said young Alexandre Cortot in a low voice. "You certainly didn't leave anything else out!"

Madeleine, who was standing nearby, clipped her younger brother smartly on the ear. "Watch your tongue, sir," she said crisply, and shot him a scorching glance.

He had been hanging around Madeleine and Mathieu, as if debating whether to play with the other boys or to stay by and play the nuisance to his sister and her fiancé. The boy had been one of the

Gloomy One's pupils, and had had more than his share of the cuffings and lashings which make a schoolroom move smoothly. No doubt he would have liked to even the score. But something about Madeleine's demeanor must have helped the boy make up his mind, for he elected the games.

"That takes care of *him*, I think," declared Madeleine with satisfaction. With one hand she contended with the breeze for control of stray wisps of hair which tried to creep from under her white cap. The blue skirt and red cloak billowed gently and required her other hand. She looked demurely up at Mathieu, but long lashes and blue eyes seemed to mean nothing to him that morning. His handsome face did not lighten. The breeze also played with his hair, and the long strands tickled his face. He brushed them back with a petulant gesture.

"Let's go somewhere else," he said stiffly. "The food won't be ready for a time, and I'm not hungry anyway."

"All right," she agreed quickly. "Let's go up over the rise and look down into the next valley. It's not very far."

They moved away up the gradual slope. Madeleine impulsively thrust her hand into his; he took it almost with hesitation.

"Take care now. Don't go far," Madame Cortot called to them as they started.

"We won't, Mother," replied Madeleine. "Don't worry about us. We're not hungry." She laughed. "Mother always says that," she told Mathieu.

Madeleine and Mathieu climbed silently to a low ridge between the two valleys.

"Why so glum, Mathieu?" she ventured finally. "Do you think I did wrong to reprove Alexandre? He needs as much as he gets—but I suppose you'd know that well enough! Anyone who has him for a pupil has my sympathy! Father doesn't hear half his impudence."

"I don't think I want to discuss Alexandre," he answered austerely.

In a few moments she tried again as they started down the other slope.

"Did you ever think when the breeze blows this long grass in these endless, everchanging rows, that it's like ranks of soldiers constantly re-forming their lines? The battle is never over."

He did not speak, so she tried again:

"The flowers scattered through are the officers trying to keep the lines straight!" She felt a little puzzled at his stubborn silence.

The breeze near the crest was strong, so they went a little distance down the other side. The picnic party was out of sight, and they had the beautiful little valley to themselves. Below, vineyards stretched off to the highway and a contorted ribbon of sluggish brown river. Beyond the river were more vineyards and hills fading indistinguishably into the distant blue massif. To the left, below them, was an old chateau surrounded by a stone wall. Once it had been the property of a Huguenot gentleman. He and his family had long since abandoned it, and the Crown had seized it.

Madeleine sank to her knees in the grass and began to pick the little blue flowers within her reach.

"They say the old Bellay chateau there is now to be a House of New Catholics," she remarked.

He did not answer.

"It seems like there are always stories going around about Huguenot children being carried off and shut up in such places. Why, a couple of weeks ago it was all over town. Cook came home from market full of it. Mother was rather excited. Then she and Father argued again about going to New York or some such place." She sighed. "Do you think anything awful like that could happen here?"

Mathieu lay on one elbow chewing a grass-blade. If he was even looking toward the chateau, he was looking through it and beyond. After a silence of some length, she tried again. There was a tiny frown between the delicate brows.

"Matheiu! Do you not feel well?"

"I feel very well, thank you."

"What *is* troubling him?" Madeleine wondered, as he remained glum and silent. Mathieu could be difficult at times, she reflected, but he also had his admirable side.

He had methodically planned each step of his rise, she knew. Attending school at Saumur, he had been one of the steady ones, eschewing frivolity, gaming, *trictrac*, crude pranks, riots, duels, carousing, debt, and all other forms of infamous conduct to which his fellow students were partial. Like clockwork he had won highest honors in the annual written and oral examinations, and he had good-conduct certificates for each year—*fort meritoirement,** no less. As the

*Very meritorious.

piety prize one year he carried off the book *Consolations Against the Terrors of Death*. And to be *proposant** in the Saumur church for two years was not an honor that came to everyone. He had been preparing the defense of his thesis when the royal edict shut the school. Not long afterward his dead father's estate had been confiscated on a technicality and he was left penniless. For three meager years he had been stranded in Saint Martin, bravely supporting himself as teacher of a miserable little beginners' school, tutor for several well-to-do families, and *chanteur*** of the church—when there was still a church. Plans with loose ends baffled and enraged him. Prudent planning and hard work should have been sufficient.

Well she knew Mathieu's plans for the future. Pastor Merson and Monsieur Cortot had made the arrangement that eventually Mathieu should wed Madeleine. Madeleine's dowry would be a good one. If the young minister could procure the pastorate he looked for and have no concern for his material wants through this advantageous marriage, then he would settle down to a life of preaching in successively larger churches, learned disputation, and controversial writing. In time he would become a highly respected leader of the church. He had no intention of burying himself in obscure parishes as his uncle was doing. The times were uncertain, and calamity might be expected to smite disorderly folk. But he was plagued with a growing sense of injustice that *his* careful arrangements should be so badly spoiled. Now his only avenue to the ministry would be by flight abroad, without possibility of return.

At last Mathieu broke the silence. "Why is Pastor Merson so cheerful?" he demanded. "He must be losing his mind. Four children, his church closed, no money, and he *picnics!* I doubt I can stand much more of this frivolity."

"Well, I suppose it's natural we should enjoy an innocent occasion together." Madeleine spoke up quickly in defense of the pastor. "There have been troubles ever since one can remember, but the Lord has always protected us. He knows what's going to happen. Now, what good does it do to worry?"

"You just have no idea of the situation we're in," he snapped impatiently. "Your parents probably keep it from you—or else they don't think it can happen to them."

*Candidate for the ministry.
**Singer.

"I'm not a *complete* fool, I'll have you know," she declared with spirit. "I really don't see what good it does to go about so sour all the time. My father and your uncle have their worries—more than we know of, likely enough—but they seem cheerful. They feel the Lord's protecting hand is over us, and they wait on Him to show us what we should do—and when."

"And while they picnic, the noose grows tighter."

She looked startled.

"How could you have any idea what it's like?" he asked, avoiding her gaze. "Daughter of the richest man in town, protected, favored. You can't imagine what it is like to have one's hopes blasted, one's plans in shambles."

"I believe, Mathieu, that I know more than you give me credit for. You are discouraged, are you not, because you can't finish your studies and you can't decide whether to go abroad or not, and you've lost your father's estate and now the teaching post? You know," she interrupted herself, "I think you let yourself be badly upset by all the little certain things going amiss, more than some might be when a great and risky venture fails."

"This is no jesting matter," he said coldly.

"I'm not jesting, believe me, dear Mathieu," she said gently. "Mathieu, you are but four and twenty. You *could* go to a seminary abroad—"

"That would mean exile forever!" he cried. "Would *you* want to leave France?"

"I—I really don't know. I don't think I would, I mean, unless I had to. We all may have to someday, you know."

There was no sound save the humming of insects and a trill from a meadow bird. The sun was growing hot; the clouds had disappeared. She gazed anxiously at him. He did not meet her eyes, but gave her his profile, with tendrils of long yellow hair blowing across the high forehead.

"You must have more confidence that the Lord guides His people, Mathieu. Look around you. Some get along quite well in spite—"

"Oh, certainly, mademoiselle," he countered bitterly. "The turn-coat, the apostate, does well indeed! Let him but preen himself in the king's uniform, no matter what he did to earn it, and all fawn on him like he was some great thing!"

Madeleine colored and dropped her eyes.

"If you refer to Armand de Gandon," she said coolly, "you do him an injustice. He is a very pleasant gentleman, and I'm sure his conduct is exemplary."

"A lackey of the Scarlet Woman, you mean! How much of a Huguenot do you suppose *he's* ever been? They've been heating the furnace seven times hotter for the rest of us, and he wanders by tricked out like a—a—"

He was glaring and shaking his finger in her face. She bit her lip.

"Really, Mathieu, I cannot permit you to speak in this way of a friend of my father. I suppose I should be flattered, for you do sound jealous. Of late it *has* been hard to tell that you cared very much for me. I don't know whether to laugh at you or be angry, but you are being *very* silly. Monsieur de Gandon passed through here for the first time in ten years to pay his respects. He had no interest in me, nor I in him. A betrothal means more to me than that. I think you owe me an apology for your surly speech."

Under her firm gaze, he faltered. "I'm sorry, Madeleine, of course, but—but you are wrong about him. He *is* interested in you and counts on those peacock's feathers to sweep you off your feet."

"Well," she said, only a little mollified, "you must entertain a high opinion of your fiancée to think that a stranger in a pretty coat could change her mind. We *have* been promised to each other for a long time now."

Mathieu turned on her fiercely. "Yes, now," he cried. "What about us?"

"Us?"

"Why do we wait this long time? You are older now, seventeen before the month is out. Do your parents wish you to be a spinster? Why shouldn't I 'imagine' things now and again?" He was growing vehement again.

"Calm yourself, dear Mathieu," she said, laying a gentle hand on his arm. "I—we didn't know you felt that way, but my father is a man of his word. He did not wish to seem to press you in your present situation or to hasten you."

He was taken aback. "*You* did not wish to press *me?*" He pondered a moment. "Then you are willing to go on, post the banns,* and marry a husband without prospects?"

*Banns were posted in a church or other place as prescribed by law, to advise the public of a proposed marriage.

43

"I was promised to you some time ago, Mathieu, and not to your 'prospects.'"

"Well, what if I took your suggestion and left the country, what about you?"

"Your wife would go with you," she said, "if she was wanted. Mathieu," she added, "you are not like you used to be when you first came here. I've given you my word. I'd never look at another though he wore Joseph's original coat of many colors. If my parents set the wedding immediately, would this cure your melancholy? As for your evil circumstances, you know God can turn evil to good."

He seemed unable to discard his jealousy so quickly.

"Well, I should no longer have to worry," he rejoined irritably.

"Then let's tell them," she said at last, without looking up. "They will be anxious only that we are happy." She feared she did not sound particularly happy just then.

He said nothing more. Perhaps he felt he had said too much already. He rose to his feet, retrieved his hat, and helped Madeleine up. They silently retraced their steps up the slope and down the other side. They could hear the distant sounds of merriment where their friends were eating dinner.

CHAPTER 3

I

TWO weeks after the great day at Versailles, Armand de Gandon descended the slope to Saint Martin on his big bay. The late afternoon sun gilded the steep roofs of the town, touching them with a golden brightness that the narrow alleys never saw. The pastel quiltwork of the fields was growing darker, and the blackish trees climbing the gentle hills to the horizon cast long shadows. The uncertain river wandered through the rushes below the walls and glowed for a few moments in an unnatural rose. Amid its rustic setting, rising comfortably above crumbling walls, the town looked like a quaint old colored print, far removed from strife and turmoil.

"And, unlike Paris, Saint Martin cannot be smelled a league away," Armand reminded his horse.

As the soldier closed the distance to the town, his weary muscles and empty stomach were ready for the welcome he could anticipate at the Cortots'. The tired horse carried him through the battered gate, where the municipal arms surmounted the arch. Sections of wall still stood behind the filled-in ditch, a reminder of the bloody days when the Protestant townspeople had resisted their king. That was sixty years before; now grass and weeds had taken over, and even the slovenly sentry was not in sight.

Armand's mount picked its way delicately over the open sewers, through refuse piles, dodging pigs, chickens, and an occasional child, to a small square. Bearing slightly to the right, the soldier rode down a narrower side street, ducking from time to time to keep from being brained by overhanging signboards. It was the quiet time of the evening. He met no adult in the airless thoroughfare, but as he was coming up to the Cortot house, he saw a small black *calèche** round the bend ahead of him.

*Open carriage.

The Cortots' massive front door stood ajar. Armand was surprised. He dismounted stiffly, for he had been in the saddle since dawn. He called and then rapped on the door panel, but there was no answer. Still more puzzled than alarmed, he entered the foyer. The house seemed deserted. Surely, in these times, if the family had gone away, they would not have left the door unbarred.

He was about to call again when he heard something like a moan. Through a doorway he saw a plain buckled shoe lying on the floor, then a stockinged foot nearby. Stepping quickly forward, Armand found one of the Cortot manservants, apparently unconscious, lying on the planking.

"What ails you, boy? Where's your master?" he cried out in alarm.

Armand knelt beside the prone figure, now stirring slightly.

"You're coming out of it now," he said encouragingly. "What's happened? Where is everyone?"

The servant began to collect his wits. He blinked several times and then tried shaking his head, but this made him groan.

"They got the twins," he said at last in a shaky voice. Armand helped him to a sitting position.

"Oh, come on, fellow. Who did? Speak up!"

"A couple of bailiffs did." The servant, now sitting unassisted, fingered the back of his head. "Got them both—Louis and Louise. Carried them off in a coach." He seemed more concerned with the lump on his head than the twins for the moment.

The soldier just remembered a coach.

"When?" snapped Armand impatiently and shook the unfortunate vigorously by the collar. "Where?"

"Had an order from the intendant, they said. Wasn't no one home but us. I never dreamed— Well, how was I to expect—?"

"Yes, yes!" snarled Armand. "Now quit babbling or I'll give you a knock myself."

"That's all right, monsieur. Needn't get so excited. You can't do nothing anyhow. They came in a little black carriage. They're taking them to the House of New Catholics out by the south gate, I suppose. Said they had witnesses the twins asked for religious instruction, and—"

As the servingman wobbled to his feet, Armand had already dashed away, leaving the door ajar again.

46

II

AS ARMAND lashed his surprised horse down the deserted street, he was overcome by a cold fury. He had not forgotten Versailles, the Duc de Lauzières, the regiment—they just did not seem important at the moment. What did matter were two frightened children. Gandon, level-headed major of the Regiment of Maine and devoted servant of the king, had vanished like a spark struck from flint. A hundred years of discipline he shed instantly, and reverted to the mind of his Bearnaise ancestors who thought nothing of drawing sword on Majesty itself in defense of the Right.

Rounding the third bend, the bay scrambling and sliding in the loose dirt, Armand saw the small black coach joggling slowly along the unpaved street. Breathing a short prayer of thanks that he was not in uniform and that no one else was in sight, he jammed his hat down on his ears and launched his mount on his quarry.

The coach was just about to take a somewhat sharp turn to the right when the horse and rider came up behind them out of nowhere so rapidly that the driver had no time to locate the direction of the hoofbeats. Armand drove his animal into the near coach horse just as they started the turn, and simultaneously brought his heavy cavalry pistol down on the nose of the surprised horse as hard as he could. The team bolted instantly. The coachman yelled in terror. Already over too far in the narrow passageway, and now crowded by this apparition, the coach had no room to turn. The fleeing horses squeezed past the jutting corner of the stone building, but the wheel of the vehicle struck with shattering force.

The axle snapped as the flimsy coach crumpled into kindling and splinters. In the middle of a shriek, the coachman shot from his seat out into the mud, where he rolled over and over to the far side of the street. The fastenings of the leather springs gave way, and the coach body dropped to the ground. For a second the coach horses plunged and kicked, and then tore loose and galloped off down the street. The driver cowered in the gutter, his hands over his head, still screaming as the animals clattered past him, their hooves missing him by inches. Back in the wreckage lay the kidnappers, stunned and helpless. Blood from an ugly scalp wound ran down the fat face of the head bailiff.

Armand slid to the ground and pulled the two children free. They had been riding backward and were only stunned by the collision. Placing them on his horse's neck, he hastily jumped into the saddle and fled. It was time, for in the crepuscular glow he had glimpsed white faces at windows. Citizens ran out of doorways even as he sped around the corner. He hoped that no one had had the presence of mind to get a square look at the rescuer.

III

"I HOPE I have not seemed inhospitable these last ten days," Cortot protested wearily, "but it *is* dangerous for you to tarry here. You know we are grateful for your rescue of the twins and your desire to be of help for Madeleine and Alexandre, but you only endanger yourself." He sat heavily on the edge of the bed on which Armand had been lying fully clothed.

"Yes, monsieur, I know," replied Armand. "We've been through this before, and I don't think you can change my mind. I'll go over your city wall some night; but no one knows I'm in town, and I may be of help. But what of your visit with the mayor? I see they didn't lock you up yet."

"It was most unpleasant. It was plain *I* did not assault the bailiffs, yet they must believe I know more than I tell. The coachman swears they were attacked by at least ten ruffians." He smiled wanly. "The curé was so furious that he stuttered, and I thought he might be called heavenward any moment by an apoplexy. He threatened the mayor with the bishop, and I think that saved me. One could see the mayor's ears go back and a stubborn look come on his face."

"Do not the town fathers get on well with the clergy?"

"I suppose so, with the curé, at any rate. They hate the orders, you know, because they are usually exempt from the *octroi*,* and that raises the taxes for everyone else. Our council fought this new House of New Catholics bitterly. They didn't need to be told who would be supporting it eventually."

"I thought," said Armand, "that the idea was to carry off children of the better sort only, so the House would pay its own way."

Cortot shook his head.

"When they carried off my Madeleine and Alexandre, they took

*City toll.

48

forty others as offerings to their idols, but since then, many families have disappeared entirely, heading for the frontiers, I don't doubt, to save the rest of their children. This puts the upkeep of the kidnapped ones they leave behind on the few of us who have means. If I go or am jailed, they'll have that much more trouble supporting their captives without calling on the town revenues. I can see the mayor's thought in this."

"Any word from Madeleine yet?" Armand rose and slipped on his shoes.

"Only that of three days ago, that she had expressed a desire for instruction and requested that we not be allowed to disturb her while she undertook these studies. She'll be permitted no visitors until she abjures, I suppose, or she will certainly be well chaperoned if we are allowed to visit her."

"A kindly thought of His Majesty. Do not disturb her, forsooth!" Armand smiled without mirth.

"At least we know where she is, but there's no word from Alexandre. I don't know where the nearest House for boys might be."

"I'm sorry my presence has been a trial to you," said Armand. "Truly, with Madame ill also, you have been sorely tried."

"I'm confident that both of my children will be true to the Faith," said Cortot, "and I'm sure the Lord knows of the wretched condition of my wife this past week. Her affliction is mainly from the shock, I think; and though I am still uneasy for her, she seems better today and will be up soon."

A knocking at the street door sent Cortot from the room. From what he could hear, Armand judged that the pastor had arrived, accompanied by his nephew, the tall Mathieu. They were climbing the stairs now, and the voices of the two older men sounded excited. The soldier grinned at the discomfiture awaiting the schoolmaster.

"We must have a secret place for what I have to tell, Brother Cortot," said the pastor. "Walls have ears these days."

"Nay, pastor," replied the bourgeois firmly, "you wrong my servants. They are part of the family. They grumble a bit, but they are absolutely loyal."

Armand looked down upon the rosy pate of Cortot as he puffed up the stairs. Behind him came the pastor in the plain black required by law.

"Come on up, brethren," urged their host. "We'll talk in Monsieur Gandon's room. He'll be glad for a chance to do something."

At the mention of that name, the head of the third man on the stairs jerked up. In spite of the dimness of the stairwell, Armand caught a glance that was even darker. "Well met, friend," he remarked to himself ironically. "Sorry to spoil your day!"

"I hope now, Brother Cortot, that we may have a way to reach your daughter," began the pastor as soon as the trio had entered the room and shut the door.

"I rejoice to hear it, pastor. Pray make yourselves comfortable, gentlemen."

The pastor perched on a stool near the head of the bed. Cortot dropped again into a chair, and the two young men sat on the edge of the bed, somewhat in the fashion of strange dogs encountering one another for the first time. The pastor gave them a long look, smiled faintly, and turned to Cortot:

"I do not delude myself that we have a sure way to Mademoiselle Madeleine, much less to rescue her. But this may lead to something."

Armand and Cortot leaned forward anxiously; Mathieu frowned at the floor.

"You remember that Petitjean who was the instrument used to bring down the temple a month ago? I have seen much of him of late, for he carries a troubled conscience for the harm he wrought the church. Yesterday he told me that he keeps company with a kitchen maid, one Lisette, at the House where the females are kept—the old Bellay chateau, not far from town."

Cortot nodded eagerly.

"I said nothing to him then," the pastor continued, "but do you perceive the opportunity which may present itself?"

Both Gandon and Cortot nodded.

"In his anxiety to repair some of the damage he has done," the pastor continued, "might not Petitjean be an intermediary, perhaps enlisting his friend in our aid?"

"It would lighten the burden on my heart, pastor, were I to hear from the girl," said the father. "But the risk would be too great."

"No, monsieur," interrupted Armand, half rising in his eagerness. "Don't use the fellow as a courier. That would be to tempt fate. Let him carry *one* message, but let it be to arrange a rescue!"

"A rescue, you say," and Cortot shook his head sadly. "That's a *very* frail vessel."

"True," countered Armand impatiently. "But we could tell Madeleine where to meet me—us. The note would say nothing of rescue. We would need Petitjean no more."

Cortot did not look entirely convinced. The pastor smiled benignly.

"Brother Gandon has anticipated my thought in the matter—"

"Not so fast, Uncle," cut in Mathieu almost rudely. "I have more reason than anyone else to see mademoiselle delivered," and he shot a meaning glance at Armand. "But this lackey Petitjean has played us false before and in his cups would easily do so again. It will be of no help to the lady if we are all broken on the wheel!"

"Mathieu is right," conceded Cortot, somewhat wilted. "It's the house built on the sands."

"No," replied Armand with a nonchalance which seemed to choke Mathieu, "they could but hang us. It's worth a try." He laughed, probably the first time that sound had been heard in the house for days.

"If I could but get her out of that House," Cortot explained, "I would send her and the twins to my cousin in Champagne. They would be safe for a time, at least, and later—well, conditions might improve here or, in any case, the borders would be closer."

"I would count it a privilege to escort them there, sir." Armand sprang to his feet and began to pace back and forth behind the men's chairs.

"I wish," sighed Cortot, "that we might free all the children shut up there."

"I wish so, too," agreed the pastor sadly. "But it would not do. They would be rounded up shortly and the worse treated for it. There are not many with your means, brother."

"God is good to us beyond our deserts," agreed Cortot.

"If this succeeds, Monsieur Cortot—" Armand stopped his pacing and looked down at the older man—"credulity will be terribly strained when a child of yours escapes twice in a row. They can play a very rough game. Have you ever been put to the question? Run, sir, and get out of the country while there is time. Even if they don't find where the twins are hidden, they'll be so suspicious of you, they'll have you locked up soon on one pretext or another."

Cortot licked his lips and his head sagged.

"Why wait? Many have passed over into the Germanies and to the Provinces of Holland—even to England," Armand persisted.

"It's as I've said before," Cortot sighed. "This is our soil. We were born here, and our parents are buried here. I grant you the brethren in those countries have been more than kind to those of us who have fled. But, well, look at England—a king hardly better than a papist himself, cold fogs, a barbarous tongue. Once you run, you must always be ready to run again." He smiled faintly. "And the place smells of coal fires, I hear."

"You are making excuses now! Have you had a whiff of the alley outside your own front door lately? Anyway, I doubt King Charles can do much to turn the minds of Englishmen."

"I know little of such matters, Armand, but what would a man of my age do in a foreign land?"

"Fie, Uncle Isaac! This is not like you." He looked fixedly at Cortot until his host dropped his eyes.

"Well, Armand," he began hesitantly. "What I tell you, you may have suspected. Madame is quite set on staying here. To her, this is faith; I hope it be not presumption. I hope, as signs multiply, that she will be persuaded while there is yet time. I wish we had our eldest boy again. He was like you—ready for action—" His voice trailed off.

"Still," added Cortot, "how could one feel safe anywhere? The king's reach is long. I have thought of the English settlements in America. I would prefer a French land, but only good Catholics may go to Canada."

His voice shook with sudden feeling. "If I could but get my family to Holland, they could have every stick of property I own, nor would I much care what they would do to me." He paused. "I've had such an easy time. So many of the troubles have passed me by. Saint Martin is one of the pleasant places, and I feel even as Lot, reluctant to flee Sodom, and it about to burn about my ears. My wife, that is—well, it is hard to know what to do. Sometimes I think one thing, sometimes another." He raised his hands in a gesture of futility.

"Then shall I broach the matter to Petitjean, with such caution as I can?" the pastor resumed. He looked sharply at the two younger men. "If mademoiselle can win free of the building itself, surely you two nimble fellows could spirit her to a city of refuge."

"Surely," Armand agreed without consulting Mathieu. "If I—we are caught, it would not be the ruin of an entire family, but just a

52

prank by addled gallants. If it is successful, I rejoin my regiment, with no one, I trust, the wiser for my sojourn here. And perhaps Monsieur Bertrand might wish to keep on going to Holland. Prospects for preachers hereabouts must be poor." He turned cheerfully to the glowering Mathieu. "Are you with me?"

Mathieu's agreement, when it came, sounded a trifle forced. "I assure you, gentlemen, that I would do all in my power to arrange for the safety of mademoiselle, for surely you understand my sentiments for her. But any plan must be drawn up with care. We must, ah—avoid recklessness and—and bravado—and plan very carefully," he ended lamely.

Armand looked at him quizzically and said nothing.

IV

MADELEINE lay on her pallet in a crowded room on the second floor of the House of New Catholics. It was pitch black, chill, and damp; but she was not shivering entirely from the cold. Outside the glassless windows, the rain hissed against the sloping tiles of the roof. It had been raining for hours, and the wind was rising. She had no real idea what time it was. Had it been ten minutes or an hour since the sister had removed the candle after her last look around the roomful of girls?

Never in her short and comfortable life had she wanted to do anything as desperately as she wished to escape from this house. It was not one of the fashionable convents where exhausted reprobates retired to tidy up their spiritual affairs before death, and indiscreet ladies might spend enforced vacations from the Court. This one was newly opened and still in some disrepair.

That it was cold and comfortless might help to break the wills of its young inmates, but it was not physical discomfort that Madeleine Cortot had quickly learned to hate and fear. Every day brought home to her more strongly what a lifetime in such a place would mean. Sometimes, it was true, stubborn cases were released in a few months if the sisters felt conversion was hopeless, but then an order from the king could shut such a one up in a regular convent for the rest of one's life—and force an endowment from a father as well. This might easily happen to her, for her father was wealthy, and she would be too valuable a prize to relinquish.

That she would suffer her faith to erode never seriously occurred to her. It was a question of living a life of unending gray, under a ceaseless drizzle of ritual and "instruction," of unrelenting pressure which at times was outright intimidation. No physical mistreatment to speak of, but unrelenting "charity," the mechanical repetition, until one was ready to go out of one's mind. The work was hard, and it was not difficult to keep one's mind numb during the day. But at night, in the dark, with a vivid imagination at full gallop, she came closest to losing her grip on hope.

Two days ago, while she was on her knees scrubbing the kitchen flagstones, Lisette had suddenly loomed over her. Madeleine, now used to the heavy hand of the big peasant woman, had automatically flinched. Lisette seemed especially to dislike Madeleine—perhaps because the Huguenot girl had the book learning and strong opinions that so scandalized the Romanists and made the heretic women more difficult to deal with than the men. Madeleine disliked almost everything about Lisette also, from her coarse red hands to her mustache, but this time her tormentor stopped directly in front of her.

Madeleine did not look her in the face, but stared instead at the heavy ankles and the purple veins above the wooden shoes. She gritted her teeth and waited for the blow, but instead, a tiny wad of paper dropped in front of her. Her heart had leaped crazily. Instantly she placed one wet hand over the paper and continued her brush stroke with the other. Lisette lumbered away without a word. A hearty smack resounded a moment later, and told Madeleine that Lisette had caught some Huguenot girl dawdling. None of the other captives or servants in the room appeared to have seen anything.

Madeleine scrubbed herself into a corner and surreptitiously unfolded the bit of paper. It was wet, and the writing was blurred and hard to read: "Be at back wall Wednesday midnight."

She caught her breath. Who could have sent it? Was it a cruel joke? Was Lisette an ally—perhaps a secret Protestant? She felt so excited that the room spun for a few seconds. She hoped her face did not betray her.

Then she had straightened her aching back and risked a glance at the square, sallow face. The slatey eyes were as expressionless as ever. Not a flicker of understanding or complicity there! "Lisette wants nothing to do with this," she mused as she resumed her scrubbing. "So be it! But how do I get out of the building?" Later, at

54

her first opportunity, she had swallowed the note, though it nearly gagged her.

The next morning she had made a special point to look out the window of the second-floor room she slept in. The windows had been hastily barred by wooden slats—sufficient to restrain young children and girls until something more permanent could be devised. Underneath the window, the tiled roof sloped off to the hillside rising in back. Over to the right a projection of the roof covered the kitchen storerooms, and here the roof came closest to the ground. To leap to the ground from there should not be too hard. Then it would be uphill fifty yards or so to a tall stone wall at the rear of the garden. Certainly there would be no way over the wall from the inside. Beyond lay the grassy slopes where only a week before she had lain in the spring sunshine and talked marriage with Mathieu. It seemed ages away now. Mathieu must be the one who sent the note. A rush of affection and homesickness swept over her. She strangled a sob and wiped two tears away quickly with the back of her hand.

The day had dragged on routinely—orisons at half past six, catechism at a quarter after seven, mass at nine. Then sessions of work and study, always under close supervision, and with silence usually imposed. Madeleine's mind kept busy, however mechanically her hands might work. If she could but lay hands on some implement to pry the wooden bars off the window!

Not until almost time for the litanies at four o'clock did she find her opportunity. She had been peeling turnips for supper, and as she turned away from the table with a panful, she pretended to trip on the uneven flagstones and cascaded turnips over the floor. She had immediately dropped to her knees to pick them up and slipped the knife she had been using inside her shapeless gray blouse. Her "accident" attracted attention, but not the reason for it, so she hardly minded the cruel slap from Lisette or the parting shove through the doorway toward the chapel.

Now she was wondering if the blade would prove strong enough after all. If it broke, that would be the end of the matter. To try to slip through the ground-floor areas, where the sisters had their quarters and the windows were grilled with iron, would be hopeless. As hopeless as trying to unbar the great front door.

At supper she choked down a little of the turnips and mashed chestnuts, keeping her eyes lowered modestly, lest anyone read her face. The Mother Superior usually seemed to be in a world of her own, but that heavy opaque gaze might take in more than one suspected. Madeleine was still dreading a last-minute summons. Was it all a cat-and-mouse game?

After nine-o'clock prayers, the flock were shepherded to their cells. It did not take the girls long to prepare for bed. They wore only the simplest blouses and skirts of peasant gray.

When the light had been removed, the girls whispered their prayers—their real prayers. They had to be careful, for there would be extra work as punishment if they were overheard. One could never tell when someone might be listening in the hall.

Madeleine lay in the dark, overcome by a feeling of meanness and misery she had never felt before. She had no assurance that she could escape, but just the hope had renewed her courage. She had felt responsible to the younger captives, who were equally frightened but understood less than she why they had been suddenly torn from their homes. What would happen to the little ones who had no hope, no outside friends? Must they stay here and be taught that their parents, their loved ones, were irremediably damned? Yet she could not organize an escape of all forty of them. This would mean disaster. Was it her duty to stay? Or to go? Would the others be punished if she escaped? Would they be encouraged or dismayed if she succeeded? She wrestled with her doubts until she unintentionally dozed off.

Now she lay awake, listening to that incessant rain and wondering if she had overslept and thus ruined all. There might be no time to lose. But was everyone asleep? Long after the faint gleam of the candle had died away, the rustlings and groanings and sighings of restless children would continue. Some were not far from nightmare; some would lie awake in the cold dark, listening to the rain and the wind as they whipped against the big house. How soon would it be safe to try the window?

The monotonous downpour continued.

"It *must* be midnight," she thought as panic seized her. "I can't stand this any longer!" She sat up and tried to see the other beds in the dark. It was as black as the inside of a boot. "If I can't hear them above this storm, perhaps they can't hear me," she thought.

Madeleine eased herself off the mattress to the stone floor and crawled toward the window, guided more by sound than by sight.

56

Twice she touched the corners of straw pallets, but the sleepers did not stir. Reaching the window at last, she rose cautiously, experimenting with the edges of the boards. Working as carefully as she could, and praying that the slight squeaks and scrapes of the knife would be drowned by the noise of the elements, she finally worked one end of a bar loose, so that the nails stood out nearly their full length from the wall. She stood and listened a moment, oblivious to the spray which had already drenched her head and shoulders. Then she began on the next bar.

When all three boards were loosened at both sides, it seemed that hours had passed, but the knife remained unbroken. There was no telling what might be waiting for her out there in the dark. A knife might be a handy thing to have. She pushed with all her strength on one side of the loosened bars, forcing the nails out of their holes, bending the boards outward on the nails of the other side as if they were hinges. When one bar screeched suddenly in protest, her heart jumped against her front teeth, and she waited a long moment before she dared breathe again. At last all three bars stood outward.

She climbed through the opening. Madeleine was taller and slimmer than most French girls, but it was not easy. The protruding nails took a heavy toll of her skirt and blouse. Standing on the tiles outside the window, she carefully pushed the bars back in place as well as she could, hoping that they might seem normal, at least at first glance. Then she turned and began to inch her way in the darkness down the slippery roof. The rain beat on her and the wind ripped at her. It blew her cap off almost at once and her hair went across her face. She was thoroughly soaked. A loose tile slithered down the slope and went over the edge. It made only the faintest plop as it struck the sodden ground below. Here was another advantage of the storm, she realized. If she should fall, the muck down there would reduce the chance of injury.

Step by step she felt her way and at last reached the edge of the roof. She explored the void with an inquiring toe. Rain, wind, and darkness blurred everything in one indistinguishable pall. The wind-driven drops blinded her, and the moaning of the wind made a nerve-racking setting for the nameless terrors lurking below.

At last she felt she had reached the extension of the roof which covered the storerooms, and went more boldly. The drop off that part of the roof would be only a few feet. Reaching the edge, she took a deep breath and, commending her safety to God, jumped, accompanied by several tiles. She landed on hands and knees in a slough formed by the runoff from the steep hillside flowing along the back wall of the building. She had hardly been jarred.

Unable to see anything, Madeleine followed the steepness uphill toward the invisible stone wall. By now she felt sure there was no trap. In the drop she had lost her knife. It was just as well, she told herself, for she doubted that she could bring herself to use it. She remembered when the bailiffs had broken into the Leblanc home and laid hands on her, she had been too paralyzed to move. Alexandre, on the other hand, had fought like a fiend until two of the officers had wrestled him to the floor and one of them sat on him. The other was nursing a very bloody nose. She wished she had Alexandre there at that moment. He had often been a painful nuisance, but she promised herself she would never speak unkindly to him again if the Lord permitted them to be together once more.

Bushes and low, swaying tree limbs clutched at her. They scratched her face and arms and completed the ruin of her skirt, now almost rent in two. A short while later she bumped into stone and knew she had gone as far as she could. Collapsing on the muddy ground, she buried her face in her soggy skirt. The rain continued to come down in sheets. A small river ran down her neck. She realized she must have cut her foot in the climb, for it was paining her now. Whether she had arrived too early or too late she did not know; she felt so tired she could hardly force her mind to consider the question.

V

FOR the fourth time, Mathieu Bertrand tripped over a root or stone and fell flat in the darkness. The storm lantern he carried flew from his hand and disappeared. The slight injury to his knees and the additional mud on his clothing were as nothing to the damage to his self-esteem, and the nonchalant bearing of his companion made it no easier.

"No matter," cried Armand de Gandon above the storm. "We're getting so close to the House now we'd have to put the lantern out soon, and in all this slop it wasn't doing much good anyway."

Mathieu said nothing as they struggled along, the wind tugging at their cloaks, the rain stinging their faces in spite of turned-down hat brims. He had agreed to this mad business because he did wish to have Madeleine rescued if it was at all possible. But he had to admit that he had been dragooned into it, partly, at least, because he was so sick of the way everyone fawned on this soldier. Certainly if everything didn't have to be done in such a mortal hurry, something more practical could have been worked out. He hadn't imagined it would be like this, blundering about blindly in a torrential downpour. He simply was not at his best in this sort of thing, and he suspected Armand knew it. But his uncle had been so anxious to push the matter.

"Let's bear a little down the slope," called Armand. "We don't want to overshoot the wall in the dark." He drew his sword and felt ahead of him like a blind man with a cane.

Five minutes more of groping and they fetched up against a wall. By stumbling along for several yards, they determined that it ran at right angles to the slope and not with it. They knew then they had the rear wall. From the outside, climbing would be no great matter. The problem would arise in attempting the return trip, for the ground falling away downhill made it taller on the inside than out. One of them would have to stay on the top of the wall to pull the other back up. Both were tall and sturdy; it would not matter which one went over the wall.

Armand seemed to undergo a sudden attack of delicacy. "Here's the rope," he said. "Jump, and I'll pull on your signal."

Mathieu froze. Perhaps Madeleine was waiting on the other side of the wall, and perhaps she was not. Who knew what might be in ambush for one foolhardy enough to drop off the wall into nothingness? Suppose the note had been discovered, or Petitjean or Lisette had played the traitor, or Madeleine had been caught and forced to talk? For a second the rain lashed at his face and he stood speechless. He could not see Armand's face, but he was certain what its expression would be—a leer of triumph or contempt. A wave of self-pity flowed over him and tears of rage stung his eyes. It was not a fair contest. He could not help feeling ridiculous.

"I imagine you are more expert at such ventures. *You* jump and *I* shall hold the rope," he said at last.

Mathieu's answer was actually prompt enough, and Armand seemed not to notice the hesitation. He needed no second urging and dropped off into the convent yard, landing with a splash that was audible above the downpour. Mathieu, teetering on the top of the wall, found himself toying guiltily with the wish that this debonair one would walk into the arms of waiting papists and *then* see what his cleverness would get him.

It seemed an age, waiting, holding the rope's end. Mathieu felt as conspicuous as though he were standing on the top of the wall in broad daylight, though it was black as the pit down there. What would that crazy soldier do if Madeleine had been unable to get out of the building? Go in after her? The very thought so stirred up his terror that he nearly fell off the wall. He was trying to master his vertigo when he felt a sharp tug on the rope. Armand, or someone, was below him now, though invisible in the darkness.

"Hold it firm," hissed the someone. Mathieu braced himself convulsively. Suddenly Armand was beside him, gasping for breath.

"Pull!" gritted the officer. Madeleine came up with the rope looped around her hands and wrists. They tried to keep her swinging in the clear, but of necessity she bumped and scraped the stones, and encumbered by the sodden skirt, had some trouble before she was atop the wall with the two men. She made no outcry when her knee, unprotected by the remnants of her skirt, was gashed against the rough stone.

Armand then dropped to the ground on the outside of the wall and Mathieu without a word grasped Madeleine's wrists and lowered her to the ground where Armand waited.

They stood there a moment to get their bearings. Armand coiled the rope. Madeleine began to cry quietly. Mathieu could think of nothing to say meet for the occasion. Each man then grasped an arm and they half carried, half dragged the girl through thickets and over rocks.

After endless weavings to and fro, they felt themselves on level ground and proceeded along the deserted highway, past the old Huguenot cemetery to a stone bridge half a mile distant from town. They crossed over, turned right, and in a few more yards came to a carriage hidden rather unnecessarily behind a screen of oaks and bushes a hundred feet from the road. A hoarse voice hailed them anxiously from the coach box.

"Did you find her?" It was Moïse, the senior servant of the Cortot ménage.

"Yes, thank the Lord!" responded Armand. "She's a bit damp but will be good as new when she can change into something dry. How do the twins?"

"They're asleep," said a new voice. A leathern flap at the coach window was disturbed, but the face at the opening could not be seen. The petulant voice belonged to Rebekah, daughter of the Cortot cook, impressed for duty as Madeleine's maid. "Dry, did you say? Monsieur is indeed witty for so late at night! If only I could be dry again I wouldn't mind being hanged."

Rivulets of rainwater were running down the sagging spots in the leather roof, going inside as well as outside the coach. Armand and Mathieu lifted the dripping girl to the step of the carriage.

"Will you both be coming, too?" asked Madeleine, pausing a moment on the carriage step, pushing a wet strand of hair from her mouth.

"I'll be with you all the way to your cousin's place in Champagne," replied Armand. "I've been trying to convince Mathieu that he'd best come, too, before all the world knows just where he's been tonight. I must mount now, mademoiselle," he said, stepping back, "and we must be on our way before every catchpoll* south of the Loire is on our scent." He disappeared in the darkness. Mathieu had not released Madeleine's hand. He tried to see her face in the darkness.

"I shall never forget your bravery, dear Mathieu," she said earnestly, "and the terrible risks you have taken tonight. I shall ever be in your debt."

"It was nothing," said Mathieu, clinging desperately to the hand. "I would like to come, of course, but I must remain in Saint Martin to allay suspicion. I do hope you understand. It would never do if we should disappear at the same time. But, I have your promise to wait for me?"

"Yes, I'll wait for you Mathieu, till the end of the world, if necessary."

He kissed her hand, while the relentless rain continued to soak them both. Almost he decided to go with her now; but to flee all across France?

"We will go on with the wedding when this furor dies down, shall we not?"

*An exactor of taxes, or other officer with power to arrest.

"Yes, dear Mathieu," she said tenderly, "but do come soon!"

Armand rode up, ready to go. Moïse, aware of the scene at the carriage step, sounded worried, cold, and impatient.

"How long are we supposed to sit here and gargle rainwater?" he complained. Armand undoubtedly had the same question, but forbore to ask it aloud.

"I cannot say how grateful I am, monsieur, for what you have done," said Madeleine. "The two of you have saved my life, and I think my reason, too."

"Our pleasure, mademoiselle," Armand returned politely. "I have been sufficiently rewarded already, but we must share your gratitude with your father and the good pastor. It would be most agreeable to remain here and converse with you both, but we are not yet safe, and there is a long way to go."

Armand turned to Mathieu. "Changed your mind about coming with us? No? Well then, *au revoir.*"

He swung his horse around. The animal was excited and hard to restrain.

"God grant you a safe journey, mademoiselle," said Mathieu. Taking her hand again, he kissed it fervently. "I will tell your parents you left in good courage."

"I pray He will protect you all at Saint Martin," she replied. "I fear what may happen when it is known I am missing. Be sure to tell my father that he and mother *must* leave Saint Martin—at once, you understand? I shall not be easy in my mind until I hear that they have gone."

"Yes, yes, I will."

"Tell them to forget the property. It makes so little difference really."

"Yes, my dear."

"You will come soon, too, won't you? We'll be waiting for you. Don't delay for anything."

The coach started with a jerk and vanished almost immediately in the gloom. Mathieu could hear it bumping and lurching along the edge of the brook as it headed for the highway.

With a heart as clammy with apprehension as his clothes were sodden with rain, he turned to mount his horse. He would ride back and forth till dawn. It would never do to rouse the guard at the gate at two o'clock in the morning.

VI

FOR the next eight days the fugitives pushed relentlessly on through the foul weather, bouncing over rocky highways, slewing through mudholes, and fording swollen streams, always wet, never stopping longer than to change horses, rarely to eat or sleep. Madeleine and the twins stayed in the coach at most of the stops, and it was the cranky Rebekah who was sent on errands for her mistress. All of the party were well worn down by the pace when they at last approached the borders of Champagne.

On that morning the sun broke through in a tentative manner and sent feeble rays through the branches of the forest aisles. Steam rose from the sodden ground and rays of light played strange tricks with silhouettes of trees and bushes. Armand, dozing over his horse's neck, repeatedly thought he saw ghostly phantasms which turned out to be imaginary when he came closer. Emerging from a patch of woodland, he spied a stream rushing over a rocky bed. The sunshine was gaining in brilliance, and the boulders along the water's edge looked dry. Surely a halt would do them all good. The twins were restless, the maid increasingly sullen. Madeleine had not complained, but Armand thought she looked haggard. What with the downpour and the fear of pursuit, they had hardly exchanged a hundred words on the journey. Armand drew in his horse and hailed Moïse.

"It can't hurt to stop a few moments in this place. There's little likelihood of passersby, and it would be good to feel solid ground again. Let's catch our breath here in this pleasant spot."

The coachman brightened immediately and without a word drove the light vehicle off the tracks which passed for a road. He leaped to the ground, and in a few moments the horses were grazing, the twins were in the reeds throwing rocks into the stream, and the maid, perched on a boulder, was nagging them in her fretful way, though neither paid her any attention. Moïse lay with his eyes closed on the moss not far from the horses.

Madeleine lay on one elbow on a canvas from the coach. Armand sat on his saddle blanket with his back to a tree, studying her profile as if trying to commit it to memory.

"It is good to see the sun again, mademoiselle," he said. "I feared it had gone out entirely!"

"I am glad, too," she replied with a charming little laugh. "I find that the whole universe is not still shaking. In that wretched coach I feared I would curdle."

"I'm sorry for the discomfort," replied Armand, smiling. "Coaches are not the most comfortable way to travel, but I hope we have outdistanced the news of your escape."

"I keep thinking of the folks at Saint Martin," Madeleine said worriedly. "I hope they are safe. The papists will be furious!"

"It depends on the zeal of the authorities. I tried to persuade your father to leave. He will be a marked man—three children missing!"

"It wasn't entirely his fault," she said sadly. "I'm so glad to be out of that—that place, but it wouldn't be worth it if anyone suffers on my account."

"Don't worry about Mathieu," said Armand. "That gentleman has nothing to implicate him, if he keeps his mouth shut."

Madeleine looked quickly at the soldier and studied his face for a moment.

"Now, don't be unfair to Mathieu. It is not his *forte* to take desperate chances. He is not a man of war, and these midnight goings must have been torture to him. I think he did admirably." A touch of defiance entered her tone. "Of course, monsieur," she added quickly, "I am most grateful to you. It was assuredly most generous of you to go to such trouble just to help a friend of your father. But Mathieu and I are betrothed. Perhaps you did not know?"

He smiled down at her.

"Had you not been, I would have been astonished."

She stared at him, uncertain what to say. He studied his fingers.

"Monsieur Bertrand seemed surly, or perhaps I should say, unhappy, on my short acquaintance with him. Is he always thus?"

"Oh, no," she replied quickly. "He is most kind and considerate always. Of course he is naturally grave and dignified, though on occasion he sings very sweetly when I accompany him on the clavecin."

"It is my unlucky star again. I have missed this treat."

Her glance was definitely suspicious this time. "Well, monsieur, I have noticed this manner you speak of, but it is only lately that he has been thus. You are not to conclude that this is his true nature. If you knew him better, you would understand and pity, not ridicule."

He made a gesture of protest and tried to speak, but she would not let him.

"Since his college was closed and he couldn't finish his studies, he's been melancholy. Then just this year they closed the little church school, too. Don't you think his melancholy is forgivable?"

Armand shrugged his shoulders. He regretted he had brought up the subject. They remained silent for a time. Madeleine nibbled a grass blade absently.

"He really should have come with us," she said finally. "He needs a new start. I know I could help him. He's so devoted to me." She looked at Armand pleadingly. "He'll be coming after us soon, don't you think? When one has suffered so many disappointments, he needs sympathy and understanding. Have your plans never gone awry?"

Armand raised one eyebrow and affected a continued interest in his fingers.

"Now and again, but some people are not in nearly as desperate a plight as they imagine themselves."

She colored and changed the subject.

"Now, what of you, monsieur? Will this affair not injure your prospects?"

"Oh, I doubt I'm in any danger." He shrugged again. "No one knew I was in Saint Martin save our friends. I'm on leave from the regiment and just happened to be passing through town when the kidnappings took place."

He found himself telling her of his visit at Versailles. Flattered by her rapt attention, he was encouraged to go on and describe the palace and its ceremonial in detail.

"You can imagine how these prospects affected me," he continued. "My father left me little but a good name, and perhaps a parsimonious nature. I grew up with our peasant children in the duck pond by our chateau. 'Chateau,' did I say? That tumbledown relic of the last century, moldering, collapsed chambers, dingy tapestries, and rushes on the floors. It was a hopeless grind to be of the country *noblesse*. My pedigree is as long as any duke's, but my mother salted her own pork and kept her own accounts. She had one fine gown— a brocade inherited from her grandmother. We wore homespun like the peasants, and I grew up on sodden meat and soup. I had a tutor for a while, but we saw little money, and what there was kept losing its value. When my mother died, my father and I gave up in despair and went back to soldiering.

"Surely, I could repair to my estate, or what's left of it after ten years under a rascally bailiff, and I could stay home and wear my tattered serge to market and proudly advertise my gentility by carrying my sword as I peddle my turnips. Or I could go off to the wars and hope for advancement."

His tone was becoming bitter.

"Advancement? Precious little these days without a patron or royal favor. All the country nobles flock to Versailles and compete for secretaryships and commissions from the royal bounty. But I told myself I'd starve before I would beg! To live around a barracks is a boring life and one can hardly exist on the pay and stay honest. But I've tried. At least it was better than that dreary farm. Now the kindness of the duke has changed it all and I haven't had to sell myself to do it."

Armand became aware that he had been talking a good deal, and stopped abruptly. Madeleine seemed much impressed and gazed at him for a long time. He detected doubt in her eye, nevertheless, and he bridled uneasily.

"Well," he said, "I did not mean to deafen you with my complaints, but what are you thinking?"

"I don't know," she replied thoughtfully, still staring at him as if seeing him for the first time. "Really, monsieur, it would be impertinence for me to advise you."

His feeling of discomfort grew, and when he met her eyes he dropped his. She seemed to see right through him—to read his doubts, carefully as he had thought he had hidden them.

"As a client of the duke, with rank and income assured," he said defiantly, "I could be of far greater service to the brethren than as an obscure officer without hope of advancement."

"What will be the good of this for yourself?" Her voice was low. Again he tried meeting her eyes, but the collision with their violet glow gave him an almost physical jolt. He wished above all things to seem unconcerned right now, but he felt flustered by her question.

"You must forgive me, monsieur," she persisted, "for presuming to speak a little plainly. Perhaps it is due to *my* pedigree that I don't know any better. It would be wonderful for you to have these well-deserved rewards, and be able to help the brethren, too; to put behind you all the vexations you speak of, yet—" She hesitated, looked at him pleadingly, and summoned up more courage. "Yet, monsieur,

I—I cannot but tremble for your soul in such a place as Versailles."

"Mademoiselle, I have tried to explain—"

Her level glance was still difficult to meet. He turned quickly to see what the children might be doing. They had stopped throwing rocks and were examining some creature they had scooped from the water.

"I suppose," said Madeleine as she sat up and stretched gracefully, "that with all this good fortune will come a consort? What are the ladies like, there at Versailles?"

"Nothing has been said about that," Armand returned, staring into the leafy branches over his head. "In truth, the ladies of the Court are nothing special except in their wardrobes and their head-dresses. Even the king abominates their headgear, which creeps higher each year; but, I'm told, he can't do anything about it." He thought of the little blonde at the *appartement* but decided this was not the time to mention her. He hastened on. "I recall when I was a youngster we could tell who we'd marry. You go to a pigsty on Saint Andrew's Eve and knock on the gate. If the sow grunts first, you'll marry a widow; if it's one of the piglets first, then it'll be a maid!"

"And is this the fashion at Versailles?"

"Truly some of the sleeping quarters are but sties; and if you'd seen some of the sights I saw, you'd vow that the sows were there, too. I've not tried my luck."

He started to rise but remained partway, kneeling beside her.

"Let's not be concerned about the harpies at Court trapping me. Rather let's see to it that I dance at *your* wedding. We ought to reach your cousin's place by nightfall, and then you'd best start writing urgent letters to that lethargic gallant of the blond locks. You might wait too long, you know," he added wistfully. "I'll give you my address, should there be need for more traveling. The regiment is stationed in Flanders now, but in May I am on detached duty to the cavalry encampment on the Saar—three thousand men under St. Ruth—for which I am glad. Most of the infantry find themselves on the Eure, landscape gardening for the palace. The royal waterworks, you know. I'll be in Flanders again afterward. You have but to call me and I am at your command—if only to dance at this wedding!"

"No," she said firmly, shaking her head, "you have done quite enough. You are most gallant and thoughtless of yourself to offer such service to one who can mean nothing to you. It would not be right to endanger you a second time."

"I wish—" the man said suddenly. "Wouldn't you like to come to Versailles for a visit? I could show you much the like of which you could see nowhere else on earth."

"It would be marvelous, monsieur, but hardly wise—for either of us."

With a sigh he rose to get the horses.

"You are certainly a chivalrous hero," he told himself, "to do so much out of filial piety. Would you have done as much if she had been homely? The witch of Endor rather than a damsel out of the Song of Songs?"

He untied his horse and poked Moïse into wakefulness with unnecessary vigor. Soon they resumed their journey.

CHAPTER 4

I

STANDING uneasily in the stuffy chamber of the town hall, the two hundred heads of Saint Martin's Huguenot families awaited the moment they had dreaded for nearly five years. Only the occasional shuffling of feet or clearing of throats broke the oppressive silence. The bare walls were decorated with a few faded tapestries, portraits of former magistrates in heavy ruffs, and a copper plate inscribed with the municipal privileges. Above the dais at the end of the hall was a painting of the city arms on wood, surmounted by a large crucifix. The table on the dais was draped with green. Chairs embroidered with the city arms were ranged in front of it in a row. Backless benches lined the walls, but none of the Huguenots were sitting. Over all was pale light enfeebled by dirty windows high up the walls.

Outside, the red roofs and the merchants' signs sparkled in brilliant sunshine. The August sky was bright and blue, but no Protestant faces reflected the brightness. In their sober best they had come in answer to a summons by the town crier. Before he could beat his drum and bray his message in more than a couple of the town squares, every household had heard the news. They must be at the Hotel de Ville at nine o'clock.

The intendant would be there to demand of the P.R.R., the Pretended Reformed Religion, that they renounce their faith at once, all together, or face the consequences. The consequences had become well known in many French communities since the day in 1681 when Intendant Marillac over in Poitou discovered that quartering dragoons in Huguenot houses was the quickest way to bring wholesale conversions. Now Saint Martin might have its turn at the *dragonnades*.*

The crier did not mention that several squadrons of the Queen's

*Persecution by dragoons.

Regiment of dragoons rode within hours of the town. He did not have to specify such details. The birds of the air told of the matter and also mentioned that six companies of the Touraine infantry were en route also, though it would take the foot soldiers longer to arrive. The French army, it was well known, was not recruited among the good angels.

In contrast to the drawn faces and drab garb of the Huguenot burghers was a smaller group, composed mainly of the intendant's staff and the churchmen, standing by the main door. They affected to ignore the unhappy audience. Resplendent in ribbons and laces, dress swords at their sides, the young aides exchanged gossip of Paris and Court, laughing and simpering among themselves as they preened their gaudy plumage.

The bishop arrived, tall, pale, aristocratic, with prominent black brows and graying temples. His iridescent reds and purples contrasted with the brown of the obsequious knot of missionaries in his wake. The scene was an old one for them, for they traveled ahead of the dragoons and performed the baptisms which welcomed the heretics back to the bosom of the Mother Church. Whether this took place before or after the ministrations of the soldiery mattered little to them. They had come to help the local priests with the extra business. Faher Chabert, exhilarated by the prospects, chattered happily with the clerics and fawned upon the bishop.

At nine, the bell in the tower rang the opening of the assembly, and before the dull throb had died away the intendant made his entrance and ascended the low platform. The tall, thin mayor, twisting nervously at his chain of office, entered. The councilmen draped in their robes of blue and violet, with gold chains of office about their necks, followed at a slower pace. They looked uneasy, though no avowed heretics had served in the city government for some time.

The intendant, a barrel in tight yellow silk and a tremendously full chestnut wig, carried a long, silver-tipped staff in his hand. His aides and the military officers ranged themselves behind him. He stared arrogantly about the room, his square face red with heat and suppressed emotion.

Several uniformed noncommissioned officers of the intendant's escort filed in last and took stations by the doors, staring insolently at the Huguenots and spraying the adjacent floor and civilians with brown streams of tobacco juice.

70

After a tense moment of silence, the mayor gave a slight nod to the *sergeant de ville,* splendid in colorful costume embroidered with the arms of the town. He rapped for order and in a quavering falsetto declared the meeting open. Then he scuttled back to safety. The mayor produced a parchment of welcome and stumbled through the loyal banalities, under the contemptuous blue eye of the intendant. The aides continued their conversation in only slightly lower tones. The clergy listened with polite condescension, but the soldiers, plainly bored, shuffled their booted feet and clanked their accouterments.

The mayor finished at last and stepped back awkwardly, almost tripping on the hem of his robe. The town council instantly retreated a step farther.

The intendant inclined his massive head in acknowledgment of the mayor's concluding bow. Then he began to speak. He mentioned a *lettre de cachet** he held from the king for his "dear and well-beloved subjects" in Saint Martin. He suggested strongly that His Majesty was offended by the misuse of the civic freedoms permitted in the municipality, and on that ominous note called on the bishop to address the assembly.

Then the bishop, reputed to be one of the better court preachers, discoursed for some time on the love of the king and the Church for their erring children. His melodious, beautifully modulated voice swelled soothingly, almost hypnotically, as he invited the heretics to humble themselves, to put behind them the error which enchained them, and to return to the fold. Then it would be well for them in this life and it would certainly improve their chances in the life to come.

No one, he pointed out, could reasonably expect a liberty of conscience which authorized equally a lie and the truth. Was it not effrontery to claim an equality for their false religion with that of Jesus Christ, which was sacred and holy? It was lonely and cold outside the Church, he reminded them. Dawn had come, dispelling the mists of error. Many of them might actually be grateful for the visit of the dragoons and missionaries, for it would enable them to be converted and yet save face. Of course the Church deplored anything smacking of violence and hoped those assembled would recognize the spirit of love in which this invitation was extended to them.

*Sealed letter, usually authorizing legal procedures.

The intendant then resumed in a different vein. In harshest tones he assured his hearers that impudent heretics who too long abused the king's graciousness were traitors to God and could hardly, therefore, be loyal to their king. If they withstood their sovereign's order and stubbornly resisted the Holy Ghost, His Majesty would consider himself discharged from any responsibility for the pains and calamities which might befall them. Those who were reasonable would be exempt from billeting for two years, and he would not permit the intractable to intimidate the wise and prudent.

Sweeping the crowd with a glance that defied anyone to answer, he turned his back pointedly on his victims and stepped to the largest chair on the dais. There he slouched as on a throne, his legs crossed insolently.

A thundering silence followed. Even the aides stopped talking and gazed at the Huguenots. Each heretic could, no doubt, hear the pounding of his own heart. All remained dumb. To his credit, the mayor was the first to recover.

"If your excellency would perhaps allow a little time for consideration, a little time for these gentlemen to discuss—"

The intendant's face crimsoned alarmingly. The veins in his forehead stood out and the tips of his moustache quivered. He struck his fist on the arm of the chair and curled the mayor up with a single tremendous snort.

"These rascals have had twenty-five years to consider and discuss!" He leaned forward as if he might bite the unhappy mayor. "Do they think His Majesty's patience is inexhaustible?"

No one spoke.

"Enough of this trifling!" he roared. "His Majesty is not interested in seeing who can be the last one to abjure!"

Still no sound.

"Conversion today or troops tomorrow," remarked an officer softly but distinctly.

"Speak up, confound you!"

There was a rustling, a stirring in the Huguenot ranks. Cortot was aware of many eyes on him. Since the transfer of the pastor, he was the moral leader as well as the head elder. It was a crucial moment. The wrong word, the reading of assent in a brother's eye, and the whole group might collapse in a panic. It had happened elsewhere. Cortot knew that many were in an agony of indecision.

Each would have to make his own decision eventually, but Cortot was determined that the Lord must not be dishonored by mass cowardice. With an unspoken prayer for the right words but with death in his heart, he replied in a firm voice.

"Our property, our bodies, yes, our lives belong to the king, and reserving but our consciences, which concern only God, everything we have is devoted to His Majesty's service."

The moment of wavering passed. The Huguenots straightened almost perceptibly and looked boldly at their tormentors.

"I've heard a lot of fine words lately," sneered the intendant when he could trust himself to speak. "We have ways of dealing with such insolence. Has anyone else anything to say?"

The group remained silent. Nothing else needed to be said. One of the soldiers by the door laughed nastily.

The intendant rose and without a further glance at the recalcitrants, strode out of the room followed by his retinue. The Huguenots dispersed with scarcely a word, each man alone with his own forebodings. As was the custom, a ringing of the bell ended the assembly. What had in other times seemed a comforting sound, now rang brazen and ominous in their ears.

II

THE Cortot household prepared for the onslaught like a fortress expecting the final assault. Isaac Cortot made his dispositions calmly, in the knowledge that most of his precautions would be useless. The better silver and a few keepsakes he buried in several spots in the garden. Not too much could be hidden, or the house would appear suspiciously bare. The family laid in quantities of fresh and preserved meats and lined up baskets of vegetables by the cellar door. Many unwelcome guests would come for dinner. Cortot summoned the servants into the parlor and began counting out silver pieces from a small iron coffer he had taken from its hiding place behind the books.

"There is no reason for you to remain here for this unpleasantness," he said matter-of-factly. "You have been good servants, and it would be no reward for your faithfulness to keep you here. I'm going to give you your wages for the next month, and then you had better be off before the callers arrive."

There were five of them. They stood silent and stricken. Moïse, majordomo and sometime coachman, recovered first.

"Nay, Master Cortot. That would be a fine thing to do, to run off and leave you and madame with these fiends from hell. Anyway, where would we go?" He shrugged eloquently.

"Moïse is right," said Sara, the cook. "There is no safety anywhere, and the Lord can protect us as well here as hiding in a ditch."

"I am grateful, my friends," said Cortot with tears in his eyes; "but I beseech you to think of yourselves and leave while there is yet time."

After a brief argument the stableboy and two maids decided to risk trying to leave town. Moïse and Sara refused even to consider the idea. Even if one could get past the guards at the gate, the countryside would be swarming with peasants looking for fugitives.

The hot August afternoon wore on. The town seemed abnormally quiet. The four remaining in the Cortot house spent much of the time on their knees. Sometimes they just sat together in the parlor taking comfort from each other's presence. They said little. Monsieur and madame both felt thankful that none of their children would have to go through the experience. If they had regrets that they had not fled in time, no one spoke of them aloud.

From time to time, Cortot read certain of the psalms for their encouragement. He had read two verses of Psalm 130 when they became aware of a barely audible humming or buzzing sound, like a swarm of bees in a warm noontide. As it grew louder, it resolved itself into a murmur of many voices, punctuated with shouts and the scuffing of many feet. Hesitating a moment, Cortot resumed his reading with only a slight tremor in his voice:

" 'If Thou, Lord, shouldest mark iniquities, O Lord, who shall stand? But there is forgiveness with Thee, that Thou mayest be feared. I wait for the Lord, my soul doth wait, and in His Word do I hope—' "

A splintering crash came from not far down the street. They looked at each other ashen-faced.

" 'My soul waiteth for the Lord more than they that watch for the morning: I say, more than they that watch for the morning. Let Israel hope in the Lord: for with the Lord there is mercy, and with Him is plenteous redemption. And He shall redeem Israel from all his iniquities.' "

Now the tramping and the shouting came nearer. The dragoons, followed by a good representation of the town rabble, were chanting discordantly, "Catholic or dead! Catholic or dead!" A heavy and continuous pounding began at the door.

Madame Cortot sat with her eyes closed and her hands folded in her lap, lips moving. "Remember," her husband admonished, " 'It is the Lord; let Him do what seemeth Him good.' " Then he leaped to open the door before it could be battered in.

He flung the door open and was almost struck by the pistol butt with which a villainous-looking dragoon had been hammering on the door. At the side of the trooper stood an officer in a red coat. He had a paper in his hand.

"Cortot?"

"Yes, monsieur."

"You are required to provide billets for me and twelve dragoons with provision for our horses until further notice. His Majesty's command. You are to provide daily expenses for me of fifteen livres, three livres each for my men. I require a bed, three chairs, a chest of drawers, commode, and a bed for my valet, according to the regulations approved by the minister of war."

The officer strode in, bouncing Cortot to one side. An orderly, with a small monkey on his shoulder, followed. A light brass chain ran from the monkey's collar to the soldier's belt.

In seconds, it seemed, the house filled with horsemen who stamped about from attic to cellar in their heavy boots. At the back door, the family dog was shot dead before he could get to his feet. The cat departed in a flash of gray, dodging several pistol balls.

The intruders set to work at once smashing open cabinets and desks in a search for valuables. They wasted no time in asking for keys, or even seeing whether such were needed.

The officer, a captain, established himself in the library and requisitioned the chief bedroom as his own. He immediately ordered dinner. The common soldiers made themselves at home in the other rooms according to their peculiar humors. They were hungry, too, and though a number of them seemed fairly well exhilarated already, they suffered from a raging thirst. Discovery of the wine cellar followed in due course. The trembling cook worked as fast as she could, assisted by blows and oaths, while Moïse and Cortot were set to work watering the horses of the visitors. Madame Cortot, a huddled brown figure in a state of near collapse, was ignored by the intruders except for an occasional rude remark.

The troopers had brought only fourteen mounts, the officer having two, but the way they shoveled Cortot's feed and hay about the stable yard and into the mud, one would have thought they were providing for an entire squadron. One sentimental drunk decided his animal was too good for the stable and with difficulty got it into the parlor, where it plunged about in fright, with sad results for the furnishings.

Awaiting dinner, several soldiers engaged in target practice in the parlor. Soon the room was filled with a haze of gunpowder and the floor littered with bric-a-brac and glass. Cortot, passing a bedroom door, happened to see a solitary cavalryman, hat in hand, his thin face tight with concentration, slashing the bed hangings into ribbons of equal width with his sword. In the room where the children had kept their toys, the floor was covered with headless dolls, trampled lead soldiers, and smashed carts. A small drum, perhaps considered contraband, lay by the door, completely stove in. The remains of Alexandre's violin lay scattered near his bed.

"At least that's one loss the boy would be able to bear with courage," thought his father.

In spite of terror and bruises, the cook produced an enormous dinner, much of which the guests deliberately wasted. Their hilarity and violence seemed to increase by the hour. The house rang with oaths in three languages, the smashing of crockery, and the splintering of the lighter furniture.

Outside in the street a gang of loafers assembled, for the looting of the Cortot mansion promised more entertainment than usual. Of course the soldiery would not allow the civilian riffraff to infringe upon their prerogatives, but the mob waited, assured that the cavalry would put on a good performance.

Cortot had to help move his furniture, bedding, and clothing into the street. His horses were brought out from the stables. Crying, "We'll rebeat your old pewter for you!" a trooper flung an armload into the gutter. An impromptu auction got under way amid much horseplay and clowning. Expensive iron chests, mattresses, and kitchenware were knocked down for pennies, while passing members of the missionary order beamed benevolently on the fun. The big black wooden chest with the experiences of the children of Israel carved on it, a family heirloom for four generations, went for three or four livres. Cortot felt like weeping.

The evening ended at last. Except for the chamber where the officer lay, scarcely an undamaged stick of furniture remained in the house. The master, mistress, and the two servants took refuge in some of the scattered hay in the stable, for the cavalry mounts had better manners than their masters. Though weary beyond description, Cortot could not sleep, but lay in the straw looking at his house dark in the pale moonlight. It seemed to be staring blindly from black, eyeless sockets. The door stood ajar, and window frames and panes were smashed. The cellar he knew was awash. From within could be heard heavy breathing, snores, and mutterings of the dragoons as they slept off the fatigue of a pleasant evening's work. Food, wine, and filth littered the floors, and some of the guests were sprawled out on the planks, oblivious to everything, including their own discomfort. It was poor consolation to recall that normally the men would have been hanged for such conduct.

Cortot suspected that worse would be coming in the morning, for if destruction did not bring him around, tortures would soon follow —restricted only by the king's limitation that none of the heretics were to be actually killed. Soldiers were known, however, to miscalculate how much of the softening process a feeble frame might be able to stand. Though several of the missionaries had looked in on his house during the afternoon, they had made no effort yet to engage him in disputation. With them was Father Chabert, who appeared to be in the seventh heaven of delight. Vengeance might be the Lord's, but His self-appointed servants found it sweet indeed to participate. While Cortot pondered these matters, Sara called to him in a low voice. In alarm he crawled over to where his wife lay, an indistinct bundle in the hay.

"Monsieur," the cook whispered with a note of panic in her voice, "listen to madame breathe! It's not right. I can't wake her. Do you suppose it's an apoplexy?"

By the faint light Cortot had to agree she looked ghastly. Something was terribly wrong. He had feared something like this. He tried to remember what he had heard of brain fevers.

"We must get her away from here before *they* wake up," he whispered hoarsely, an icy hand clutching his heart. "This ruination has been too much for her."

"There's no place to go," whispered Moïse, who had come up silently. "All our people are in the same fix."

In his mind Cortot ran up and down the street. The most hopeful prospect might be the Delarge sisters. They were maiden Catholic ladies at the end of the street, always good friends, but it would be asking much to shelter a Huguenot woman, with these devils loose. There was no use taking her to any Protestant house, and they could not get her out of the city. He, at least, had better be here in the morning to make explanations for Mathilde. If she was dying, he knew the priests would keep him away from the bedside, but she could hardly be in worse case than she was lying here. If the Catholic ladies had sufficient courage to take her in, they would still have to report her, but so would any doctor or apothecary he might summon.

Cortot made his decision quickly. With a word to the others, he slipped out and down the alley to make his appeal. For himself, he decided as he warily crept from shadow to shadow in the deserted street, he would die before he would beg for help. But for his dear Mathilde, if he could find any help, pride no longer mattered.

III

WHILE assisting Sara with the debris after the morning meal, Cortot was waited on by a surly dragoon who ordered him to report at once to the officer. Wiping his hands hastily on his breeches, the Huguenot hurried to the library.

For several moments the great man studiously ignored him. He pretended to be wrapped up in lighting his pipe, a long church-warden, using for a spill a page out of one of Cortot's devotional books. The officer had a handsome, aristocratic face and was evidently of gentle breeding; but his mouth was thin and cruel, and the eyes as sympathetic as stones. His monkey sat on his shoulder, shrilling jungle talk and crumbling a biscuit on the floor. The officer was at his unbuttoned ease, though he wore his spurs this early in the morning, as the scars on the tabletop bore witness. He wore a ruffled white shirt and blue breeches. A magnificent red coat with huge blue cuffs and silver buttons was draped over a candelabra. On the table lay his white *jabot* and his red stocking cap with blue trim and long white tassel. Finally he deigned to notice his host.

78

"We are not swineherds, my good man," he drawled softly, "and we do not wish to eat like swine. Kindly convey my compliments to your cook and inform her that if she serves us any more of this refuse, I shall have her basted before her own fire, and you, too, for good measure. At first I thought it was a plot to poison us, but now I am inclined to credit it to provincial cooking. Now, pay attention while I place my order for dinner. I am in no mood to sample the delicacies of the region—these mashed chestnuts and such fare." He shuddered delicately.

For a long moment the captain sat and thought, as Cortot stood silently.

"Let us see this time that the table is properly set," began the officer, shaking the ashes of his pipe onto the carpet. "Bread and knives to the left, napkins to the right. Then let us start with a soup, let us say a *potage* of finely hashed chicken, distilled with barley, dried roses, and cinnamon. There will naturally be hot and cold *entremets*,* which, trusting soul that I am, I will leave to you. As for the entrée, I can't really decide between a suckling pig, or should it be spiced duck, or perhaps pheasant, or maybe partridge in cabbage?" He paused to think the problem through. "Well, then let's have them all. It will be less trouble to decide. Serve the roast with oranges, naturally, and I prefer my sauces flavored with rose water. There will be fruits in season, hors d'oeuvres—shall we say roast beef spread with kidneys, onions, and cheese—and desserts, a good variety to choose from."

Cortot stood again for a time silently waiting for dismissal. He was trying desperately to remember all that he had been told. The officer suddenly looked at him as if seeing him for the first time.

"You know, of course, that I have eight more men coming here shortly. Several of your more intelligent confreres have already seen the light. The dull ones like you will have the honor of more and more of my splendid fellows until you also achieve wisdom."

"May I ask you, monsieur," said Cortot with a sudden boldness, "do you not think it sacrilege that we are asked to abjure, and accept the solemn mysteries of your religion without sincere belief?"

The soldier jumped as if stabbed. He bared his teeth in a snarl.

"If I heard you correctly, you heretic pig," said he in his softly menacing way, "you have a truly imperishable crust. It sounded like

*Side dishes.

you were questioning the will of His Christian Majesty. I hope that I have misunderstood you, for otherwise I should feel an obligation to run you through. Pray do not bother your pretty head about such matters. If the king wishes us to convert you to Mohammedanism, we will do so. In fact, we shall labor with you folk until the sight of a single horseman will send you running to abjure. We have all the time in the world; we'll work with you until you comprehend."

"With God's help, *that* I shall never do," said Cortot firmly but respectfully.

"You have a pretty good opinion of yourself," sneered the captain.

The conversation languished. The house was not exactly silent, however, for from the other rooms could be heard loud argument and a scattering of pistol shots. Suddenly the house trembled. Two quarreling troopers were rolling down the stairs locked in each other's arms. The officer blinked and raised his eyebrows.

"Are you still here, civilian? Your presence is making me unwell. Be so good as to remove yourself at once and carry out my orders exactly and immediately. None of your stingy merchant's tricks! I know you take me for a kindly sort, foolishly indulgent and easily imposed upon, but I warn you, pray do not trifle with my natural good nature!"

Accompanied by a blear-eyed trooper, whose slight stock of French words had a strong Westphalian overlay, Cortot set off for the market. His escort unsheathed his saber, but Cortot knew better than to try to run away. He was sweating profusely, and not entirely because of the warm morning.

Cortot made his rounds with the shaggy and unclean shadow unpleasantly close behind. In some shops he was grossly overcharged by proprietors who leered at him knowingly; others gave him frightened looks of sympathy. A baker impulsively thrust several extra loaves upon him with a wordless grimace of understanding.

Soldiers, both horse and foot, filled the streets of Saint Martin. Sometimes they were shepherding miserable civilians to the church at sword point. Many of these Cortot recognized as friends and neighbors. Most were the worse for wear. As the saying went: "Twenty-four hours from torture to communion." A bedraggled Petit-jean trotted by unseeing, with a pitchfork at his backsides and once again an apostate. The brethren were crumbling, Cortot noticed with a sick feeling in his stomach, but he could not find it in his heart to blame them. There was nothing like a long summer evening with the dragoons. Eventually, after all had been ruined or devoured, the soldiery would move on to fresh victims. The bishop and his assistants must be very busy.

Cortot wished that some outstanding phenomenon might occur to mark nature's outrage at this treatment of God's faithful people. But the sky was clear and beautiful. "I must be steadfast," he told himself. "No matter what man may do to the body, the soul is to be saved. I shall be reunited with my children in the next world, if not in this one. We are not tempted above that we are able to bear," he reassured himself once more.

His meditations continued: The children must win to a foreign land. Mathieu had gone south with his uncle, but surely at the first chance he would be going to Madeleine and the twins. Madeleine would be almost penniless now, but that would make no difference to a splendid fellow like Mathieu. He thought also of Armand and was grateful he had escaped from Saint Martin. He would probably have got himself shot and to no purpose. He recalled the young man's tales of his prospects at Versailles and breathed a prayer that the soldier would prove worthy of his Huguenot father and not succumb to the snares of the world.

The trooper and his victim passed the Delarge house. Cortot stopped suddenly. The dragoon pricked him brutally in the back with the point of his saber and drew back his foot for a hearty kick. Cortot hastily dropped his bundles in the street and emptied his pockets. The soldier greedily accepted the handful of copper and silver.

At Cortot's knock, one of the sisters timidly peeped through a little crack and opened the door a full six inches when she saw who it was.

"Oh, monsieur," she cried and burst into tears. The fear Cortot had been resolutely pushing out of his mind all morning suddenly leaped to the fore.

"Please, madame," he begged in a strangled voice, "I have so little time. Control yourself, I pray you. Is she—how is Mathilde?"

The Catholic woman made an effort, wiped her face with her apron, and glanced fearfully over her shoulder. She spoke rapidly, hardly above a whisper.

"We've done everything we can, but she's very poor. She breathes harshly and all the signs are bad. The doctor has been here, and she has been bled and purged. We have shut the room up tight so no air can get in, but he shakes his head. The apothecary has been called, and he has chopped up two puppies and they are on the boil with the other ingredients for apoplexy, but they must seethe for twelve hours and—and I fear she won't last that long, monsieur. And I can't let you in. You know it's strictly forbidden. The friars came. The doctor told them. Please don't blame him, monsieur. You know the law about sick heretics, and they are with her now, but she has been unconscious all the time."

"I thank you, Madame Delarge, and your sister, for your great kindness. Heaven will reward you. I will go. I want to cause no more trouble for you."

The trooper was nowhere in sight, and the stricken husband went on to his house without him. It was an impossible thought to accept, but he knew that he would probably never see Mathilde again. He knew what the law prescribed for the bodies of dead heretics, and tried not to think of that either. "If she must go," he prayed, "Lord, let her go without regaining her senses." The missionaries would be waiting to hound the dying woman to abjure her religion to save her immortal soul. He stumbled up to his back door, his heart a leaden lump in his chest. The soldier was still missing. Probably drinking up the *pourboire** in the nearest cabaret. The gray kitten approached timidly and rubbed against his calf.

"Did you come back?" he muttered as he fumbled with the door. "Leave while you can, poor beast. You'd best abjure, Protestant pussy, and learn to meow to St. Gertrude. She's the patron saint of cats, they tell me."

He stopped. "I must be out of my head. I'd best pull my wits together; it bids fair to be a grim day."

*Tip.

CHAPTER 5

I

"THE 'Fence' will soon be down, in my opinion," said the white-haired man with the harsh voice. "The preparations are about complete, I'm told."

Jean Claude, once called by Louis XIV "the best preacher in my kingdom," wiped his mouth with his napkin. It was Sunday in October, 1685, at Charenton, the nearest Huguenot church permitted Parisians. The Arbaleste Inn was filled with the clatter of crockery and a mannerly hum of voices as the faithful consumed the noon meal between services of their largest temple.

Pastor Claude was an unprepossessing man, neither brilliant nor dramatic in manner, but his skill and vigor in debate had made him the best-known Huguenot minister. Ever since his collision with the redoubtable Bishop Bossuet, he had typified the defense of the Religion better than either of the Ruvignys.* Now he sat in a large chair with his fingertips together, frowning over his spectacles. His plate lay empty, save for a neat pile of bones. His table companions, preachers save for two, were dispatching the last morsels from the nine or ten platters before them. Most diners in the room were also subdued in color of clothing and in manner.

Pastor Jean Merson leaned forward with his elbows resting on the table. "Do you suppose I will have time to return to the south ere it happens?"

"It would be something of a risk," replied Claude in his judicial manner. "It's no secret that the Chancellor Le Tellier is failing rapidly and is using every argument to compass our undoing before he leaves this world. Louvois, as a dutiful son, and Madame de Maintenon are also said to be working with him for an end to the Edict."

" 'Where the devil cannot penetrate, he sends an old woman,' " quoted a plump pastor from Normandy in a most profound manner.

*Official Protestant commissioners at the Court.

"No one can claim it is a surprise," sighed a cadaverous minister from Picardy. "The 'Fence' has had missing planks for a generation, and they pull out more each year." He pushed his plate away gloomily.

Claude nodded grimly. "If a revocation is coupled with measures to muzzle the ministry, then our public work in France is finished."

Armand de Gandon, in civilian clothes, silently nursed a glass of lemonade and followed the speakers with his eyes. Except for an elderly deacon, he was the only layman at the table and felt tongue-tied in the presence of so much gravity. Pastor Merson had spied Armand as he entered the inn and had insisted that he join the ministers at their table.

"You are recently from the south, Brother Merson." Claude turned to the slender figure on his left. "There have been strange tales out of Nimes, my old church. Are they true?"

"I know not what you heard, but the news is bad," replied Armand's friend, shaking his head. "Pastor Cheiron preached a vigorous appeal to stand fast, and the congregation protested its determination with groanings. Yet when the soldiery appeared a few days later the collapse was general; and, though I regret to have to say it, the pastor abjured with most of his flock. It is said that after Bâville threatened them of Montpellier, eight thousand bowed the knee to Baal."

The other ministers looked stunned. "The end of all things is truly near," whispered one.

"It is the falling away foretold for the last days," agreed another.

Armand spoke timidly: "The king has sent Bourdaloue, his best court preacher, to exhort the New Converts at Montpellier. The king has said that his own courtiers would not mind mediocre sermons, but that the heretics expected sermons with good doctrine and well-presented."

"A dragoon makes a better apostle than the best court preacher," said Merson.

"We teeter on the edge of a precipice," said Claude. "It has been months since we have been able to deliver any sort of protest to the king, and the old commissioner has been told plainly that no more of our addresses will be received. The bishops who surround the throne denounce the Edict day and night. The Bishop of Albi said —and I think I quote him correctly—that it is 'the most cursed edict imaginable by which liberty of conscience was allowed to each and all; the worst thing in the world.' Of course Pope Clement VIII said this eighty years ago."

The deacon, a little man with a watery blue eye, shook his head. "I'm sorry to have lived to see this day," he quavered. "I remember when I was a boy, back in 1621, when the first Charenton church burned. What a calamity we thought that was, and like the elders of Israel, I always held our present building to be inferior to the old one. But how precious this one seems now!"

"God defend us!" said one of the others.

"Amen," agreed another.

"We live in the fearfulest age Christians have ever seen," another pastor said sententiously.

"Would you counsel one to stay for the afternoon service who must be in Paris tonight?" Merson inquired. "I am told it is not wise for those of the Religion to be out together after dark these days."

Claude, who was eating chunks of cheese off the point of his knife, took his time answering. He looked to see where the waiters were and lowered his voice.

"I do not know that we shall ever worship here again after today, brethren. The hour is even later than we think. We are privily warned that next Sunday the congregation will be filled with worshipers ostensibly one with us, but it is plotted that royal officials will appear and urge us to join peacably with the king's religion. Whereupon these interlopers will set up a cry of 'Reunion,' that haply we may lose our heads and embrace the papistical confession *en bloc.*

"If we determine this is indeed on foot, it would be better to close the church today than to have the last service marred in such fashion." He turned to Pastor Merson. "Do not be overly concerned about the police. La Reynie has arrested a few in Paris, but he is first a policeman and no fanatic. He keeps several of us in the Bastille at a given moment to prove he is properly zealous, but let us all remain for the Communion this afternoon."

After the murmur of assent, one diner arose, made his reverence, and replaced his hat.

"It is about time for the first bell," he said. "Would you excuse me. I should like to stop by the bookstore." The others rose, bowing and shaking hands. As the men passed out of the inn door into the sunshine, beggars clustered around seeking alms.

"They'll have changed their tune by next week," remarked Armand to Pastor Merson. "Likely they'll be crying in the name of Our Lady by then."

The old deacon tugged at Armand's sleeve.

"Do you return to Paris tonight, brother?"

Armand nodded.

"Then might I impose upon your good nature and ride with you? What Pastor Claude says of the police may be all very well, but I have seen too much of late to feel bold." Armand's size and armament were comforting.

"I would be honored by your company, brother," said Armand politely. "I have been to Paris several times, but I am ashamed to say this is the first time I have worshiped at Charenton. You can show me the best route to the city."

"Then shall we meet at the outside gate after the last service," replied the deacon with evident relief. "We should be able to reach the barrier by closing time." He bobbed a quick bow and hurried up the avenue.

Pastor Merson waited until the deacon had gone and then guided Armand to one side of the stream of worshipers moving up the wide paved street to the temple. They turned off on a path leading to the cemetery of the nobility.

"Well met, Brother Armand," said the pastor. "You are in health?"

"Yes, thank you, pastor," said Armand. "It was a pleasant surprise to meet you here. Have you any particular news of the south—of Saint Martin? I know nothing except that the dragonnades reached there two months ago."

"It is not a pretty story." The older man shook his head. "I am no longer there, as you know, but I passed through about two weeks ago on my way here. The brethren suffered cruelly in body and goods, and, I fear, some also in soul. Madame Cortot is dead, poor woman. She was felled of an apoplexy. Brother Cortot is in greatly reduced circumstances, but I marvel at his good courage. His house was well-nigh destroyed. When he is less closely watched, he hopes to escape from the country. Madeleine and the small children are yet in the refuge where you left them last spring. Nothing recent has been heard of the older boy who was in the House for New Catholics. Our brother's great worry now is that harm may befall Madeleine and the twins before he can arrange for their escape."

The pastor glanced at the soldier's impassive face. "And how does it with you, brother?" he asked softly.

"Well enough. One exists." Armand felt his reply was a little lame. The pastor did not press for details.

"I pray the Lord will bless you and your plans." Was there a hint of reproof in the tone? Armand dropped his eyes and was carefully noncommittal.

"Your nephew, Mathieu Bertrand? How does he? I had understood he was affianced to Mademoiselle Madeleine and was to join her ere this."

"He went south with me to Cette, but is presently near Nimes. Poor lad. He has taken our reverses much to heart. At present he hesitates to go on with the marriage." Merson sighed. "I would I might inspire him with more hope, but there is indeed little surety for God's people in these times."

The temple bell began to ring slowly, as if for the last time. The two turned back toward the main thoroughfare. Armand was deep in thought, and the pastor eyed him speculatively. They walked in silence until they were joined by Pastor Claude. Armand dropped back politely and bowed his leave-taking.

"It was most agreeable to have the honor of your acquaintance, messieurs," he said, "and you were most kind to permit me at your table."

"The pleasure has been ours," Claude assured the officer. "You must make my home yours whenever you are in Paris."

With further civilities they parted, and Armand backed into the throng and was lost to sight. With a quizzical look on his face, Merson watched him go.

"Well, old friend," remarked Claude with an uplifted eyebrow. "You look pleased with yourself. Have you performed your good deed for the day?"

"Yes, I think I have," replied the other with a satisfied smile.

II

IT HAD been a good Sabbath at Charenton. After three services, which included the reading of thirty-two chapters of Scripture, the delivery of 167 pages in three sermons, the singing of nineteen psalms, and the recitation of 200 verses, the worshipers departed satisfied. Armand found the old man at the agreed place, and they turned their mounts toward the capital. When they reached the open meadow, the horses settled down to an easy trot. Armand perceived that his companion wanted to talk. There were worse ways of spending a late autumn afternoon. Already the browns showed in the landscape, and there was a nip in the air.

"It's hardly to be believed," the deacon reminisced, "that this may have been my last trip out here. I've come by land or water these sixty-five years, sometimes twice a week. I know every foot of the way. I'm seventy-six, you know.

"Paris has always hated the Reform. I've wondered if it be Rome or Paris that is the Scarlet Woman, for the cup of filthiness can certainly be filled in Paris, too, and she is bespattered with the blood of the saints. She burned Louis de Berquin at the first, and then there was St. Bartholomew's Day. Even now our services may not be held in the city limits, but I suppose insult is better than murder.

"It's two leagues from the Bastille to Charenton," he went on, his eyes far away. "On a Sunday there would be three or four thousand come to a service. Some of us would ride, a few in carriages, but a lot more by shank's mare. Hundreds came by river. We had trouble once in a while at the *octroi** when entering or leaving the city, but the roads were more trouble—mud in the spring and slush in the winter—so it was hard on the old, no doubt; but it was great adventure when one was young.

"Long ago, the seigneurs would race their carriages—oh, the excitement! We behave more seemly now—the times are so bad, perhaps, and the nobility have fallen away. I remember once the Duc de Guiche tried to kidnap the beautiful young widow, Madame de Harambure, she was, on her way to church. Richelieu himself put a stop to that one.

"I remember how we boys preferred the river route. Only a *sol*** it cost for the trip—two hours it took—with sixty in a barge. The riffraff on the Ile de Notre Dame might pelt us with stones when we passed under the bridges. You never knew.

"How we used to sing on the river! I can hear it yet! In the fog we could hear them coming—until four years ago an edict stopped singing even in open country. The fog was dangerous. I remember

*Boundary where local taxes are collected.
**A French coin worth about a penny.

88

once a collision during the seventh verse of the ninety-second psalm. Some had to swim for it that time."

He fell silent for a time, revisiting a world peopled by friends long since dead.

"Great men, men of renown, were common in those days. Any pastor could handle an entire book of the Bible for a sermon—none of the sickly custom you see in some pulpits today of confining the Word to a few chapters. . . .

"You saw the temple today. Have you ever seen the like in all your travels? I wouldn't think so. It holds 4,000 on the three floors with the balconies; yet all can hear perfectly. And it is well lighted with those tall windows—eighty-one of them." He fell silent again.

"Truly," he sighed at last, "we shall never see the like again this side of the heavenly city." He began to recite in a high, thin voice:

> "Now as the Ark was saved from the Flood
> When God placed His Church there for safety,
> As also saved by receiving the Church
> Was little Zoar, hard by Sodom,
> So God will keep Charenton
> Under His wing."

Armand turned in his saddle. "And do you plan to flee Sodom?"

"It is much on my mind. If the Edict is revoked, it may be too late. There are many ways, though, that one might try: by land over the frontiers or by sea to England. From Paris to the Lowlands is the most direct, but the water journey is usually easiest. In any case, it is dangerous."

"I beg you to discuss these possibilities with me."

For some time they discussed the various routes to Protestant countries, by land and by sea, disguises, forged papers, guides—honest or rascally, but indispensible nevertheless—venality of frontier guards and sea captains, and the dreadful penalties on those taken in flight. They were now passing the country houses of the wealthy Parisian bourgeoisie, and the villages came closer together. Paris was near. Armand, both intrigued and aghast at his companion's disclosures, loosened his pistols in their holsters and made certain that his scabbard was swinging clear.

"It seems then," mused Armand, "that from Paris the best way is to head for a Channel port, but what if one had to start from Champagne?"

"Then such a one should strike for the nearest border. It would be well to avoid the thicker parts of the Ardennes, but one should also keep in mind that to arrive in the Rhine principalities is not always to win safety, for our troops range far into the Empire and those petty princelings dare not protest. One must have a guide and, with a good one, to head for the Netherlands might be wiser. When fleeing, one should avoid towns and villages like the plague, but circling around through forests and thickets requires a guide unless you know the country well. It is hard to say how long the border guards will remain as complacent as they have been until now, so good passports and a letter from a bishop attesting one's orthodoxy are very useful."

"How does one come by such trifles?" asked the soldier as they neared a gate.

"You are serious?" asked the old man, lowering his voice.

"Well, yes," said Armand, after a little hesitation. "Not immediately, perhaps, but in a month or so, after some arrangements have been made."

"Who can tell what the situation may be in a month?" muttered the old man out of the side of his mouth, his eyes on the guard. They passed unchallenged through the gate. "But it may be that long before I myself can go, and if I am yet here, I may be able to be of service to you. I will tell you where to find me. But, I implore you, be discreet, for these are troublous times, and among the flock are ravening wolves in sheep's clothing."

Saying no more, they fought their way through the holiday crowds in Sunday serge, past the wine and lemonade shops, shoving aside brazen-voiced peddlers and beggars, cringing as a coach driven by a madman plummeted down the narrow lanes with no regard for the lives of foot passengers. Armand saw the deacon safely to his little basement shoe shop and once again edged his cautious way through the pullulating humanity to the safety of the Duc de Lauzières' town house, more than ready for a good meal and a soft bed.

III

ARMAND DE GANDON stretched his weary legs while his horse was led to the watering trough by a strikingly unclean urchin. It had been a hard and boring week in October out on the Eure, where the infantry of France dug ditches for their king's waterworks that would eventually make his gardens at Versailles bloom. Armand had ridden in to Paris with routine papers for the duke, his colonel. He was tired and the horse was hot, so he paused after entering the gate.

He bought some raisins from the least noisy of the street peddlers who thronged about him and, ignoring the maledictions of the others, strolled toward the window of a printseller to see what was new. He was feeling quite cheerful in spite of the tedium of his current duties. In the past month of shovel work, the regiment had lost only thirteen by desertion, six dead of the fever, and scarcely thirty men in the hospital. True, the duke did not much concern himself with such matters, that being what he had professional officers for, but Armand felt a solid sense of satisfaction for a job well done. It would not be long now, surely, until his commission for the new regiment came through. He felt he deserved the promotion.

His face and spirits both dropped as he saw a royal proclamation on the wall of the shop. Grimly he read the opening words: "Louis, by the Grace of God, King of France and of Navarre, to all to whom these presents shall come, greeting. The King Henry the Great, our ancestor of glorious memory—" At last the Fence was down!

The proclamation declared the Edict of Nantes revoked, since "the greater part of the Pretended Reformed Religion" had embraced the true faith. The Edict was therefore useless. All ministers of the P.R.R. must be out of the country within fifteen days, all Huguenots who had previously fled must return in four months, and any who tried to flee in the future would be consigned to the galleys for life if men, or loss of body and goods in a convent if women. No meetings could be held. All Huguenot children born hereafter must be baptized in the Roman confession, but otherwise those not yet converted were not to be molested "until it pleases God to enlighten them like the others." At the bottom of the sheets it concluded, "For such is our pleasure," and was signed "Louis," followed by the chancellor, Le Tellier, and *"Par le Roy,** Colbert."

Furious, Armand urgently elbowed past an unsavory saleswoman for chestnuts, in order to see in the printseller's window. He needed a moment to control his emotions, but the sample in the window was no help.

*By the king.

The engraving entitled "The Pretended Reformed Religion at Bay," showed a very ill person, evidently Huguenotism, on a bed with a horrible dragon lurking underneath. A doctor was taking the patient's pulse, and a man busied himself raking Protestant books into a fire.

Several doggerel verses were included, of which Armand scanned the last two:

> Your books and your writings are burned on the spot,
> Error and heresy are reduced to ashes;
> The sun which shines uncovers to your eye
> The naked truth, your greatest enemy.

> The worship of your gods is abolished,
> The thunder and lightning which smash your altars,
> Your idols stricken, your temples demolished,
> Are the eternal witnesses of your entire ruin!

Grinding his teeth, Armand glanced at the other. It showed a grim Louis XIV brandishing a sword over the ruins of Huguenot temples. "Not without cause does the king carry the sword—" This was supported by some close theological argument: "Heretics! If you still doubt the Most Holy Sacraments, listen to Jesus Christ, for St. John, chapter six, says 'I am the LIVING bread—!'" The fine print was hard to read through the streaked glass.

Armand turned back to his horse, his mind seething with half-formed intentions. Certainly it was dangerous for Madeleine to remain in the country, yet it would be a desperate matter to try an escape now. Was it not Mathieu's affair anyway? The Revocation specifically said that Huguenots who kept their mouths shut should not be bothered until it pleased the Lord to enlighten them. The regiment would soon be his, and the duke had been trying to encourage him in a tender interest at court. There were some indications that the lady, though of highest birth, might be a little interested herself. Was it sensible to throw everything away now for a sentimental gesture—and for the fiancée of another?

He took his horse's bridle, checked his saddlebags, and for good measure felt to see that he still had his purse. The barefoot urchin held the horse while he mounted. There was something about the impudence of the boy's expression which reminded Armand of Alexandre Cortot. Though he did not wish right then to be reminded of Cortots, perhaps it was to stifle his conscience that he put the deniers back into his pocket and threw the boy an entire sou instead.

IV

THE November fog had lifted to treetop level as Mathieu Bertrand, cold and wretched from his long journey, jogged down a poplar-lined avenue. He hoped he was nearing Hauterive, the country house east of Troyes where Monsieur Cortot told him he would find Madeleine. Around his waist, concealed by his black jacket and riding cloak, was a leather belt which contained just about the last coin Cortot had been able to scrape up.

As Mathieu's nag shambled along between the dripping trees, he recalled his joy at receiving the letter from Cortot. Now, hunched over the neck of his Rosinante, he wondered what had possessed him. When the Edict had been revoked, he and his uncle had lost everything, and the latter had been expelled from France. Now Mathieu found a starveling livelihood as a clerk for a New Convert draper at Nimes. The royal net had large holes in places, and a small fish like Mathieu was not disturbed. Cortot's urgent appeal had been welcome, he admitted to himself, as an excuse to break away from a futile trade; but with this northern damp chilling one to the bone, courage also froze, and even the dusty draper's shop could be seen to offer advantages.

Mathieu viewed the future much as he did the road ahead of him now—as obscured by wisps of uncertain fog. When a vision of Madeleine's face flashed through his mind, the dimness dissolved; but then when he dwelt on the precarious prospects of one's daily bread, all became murky again. If only they had not made that fool rescue from the convent, he and Madeleine could have settled discreetly on her father's land and waited for the storm to pass. Officially, Protestantism might no longer exist in the kingdom, but in fact, each made his own terms with Caesar. The zeal of officials, the fanaticism of the clergy, and the spitefulness of neighbors varied from place to place, but a heretic who did not outwardly defy the law was not likely to be disturbed. For safety's sake, Mathieu had sent no messages either to his uncle in Holland or to Madeleine since the Revocation.

When Mathieu had located Isaac Cortot, he found him existing with Moïse and the latter's sister in a cottage in the foothills two leagues from Saint Martin. It stood on an eroded little plot with a few vines and fruit trees and a great many weeds. It had once been a herdsman's hut and a minor part of Cortot's properties. He had given it to Moïse after the dragonnades, hoping the property was insignificant enough to escape the cupidity of the enemy. His town house had been confiscated shortly afterward for "taxes," and he had slipped away to live with his former servant, trusting that he had been forgotten in town.

"How fortunate that I was able to reach you!" Cortot had cried over and over again as he embraced Mathieu. Mathieu had been shocked to observe how much the older man had aged in the three months since he had seen him last. The face once so round and rosy was heavily lined, and the wattles hung loosely. "I doubt I will ever see my children again in this life," Cortot had said. "The fury of the persecutor will not be satisfied until I am in the grave, like my dear Mathilde." The tears stood in his eyes and spilled down his cheeks. "But the young ones must make their escape from Babylon, even if they take away but their souls for a prey. Lord willing, I may try later, but it would be madness now. But this is what I wrote you for, my dear Mathieu!"

In his money belt Cortot had almost three hundred livres in gold and silver coins. He had pressed it into Mathieu's hands. The younger man's heart had beat suddenly faster as he divined what this was leading to.

"This I hid from the dragoons, my boy. Go up to Champagne. I will give you the directions. Madeleine and the twins have been there six months now, and I don't know how much longer they will be safe. I grieve that matters have worked this way, my son—indeed, I had hoped you would be my son in truth ere this, but the Lord in His providence has planned all for our good. You will no longer be marrying the daughter of a rich man. You will have only my blessing. But you are young and of good courage and you love each other; and with this, all may be accomplished. You will take your abode in a foreign land, but take heart from Ruth the Moabitess. I have a few more livres with a banker in Amsterdam, and Madeleine has my letter of credit. It will help, but my children will still have to labor for their bread. But I trust the Lord's arm is not shortened, nor does He need silver or gold. 'The Lord giveth and the Lord taketh away; blessed be the name of the Lord.' "

Mathieu had not forgotten the still-sturdy figure standing by the doorway of that windowless hut as he rode down the path toward the highroad. "I hope that you children will enter the terrestrial Canaan," the old gentleman had said, "but at least we shall surely meet again in the heavenly. I shall be forever in your debt for this service."

The long journey on a poor horse had fatigued the spirit as well as the body. Constantly on Mathieu's mind were the threats in the Revocation edict—galleys for men and convents for the women who tried to flee the country. He had heard a good many escape stories: the journey by sea hidden in bales of merchandise, or drifting in an open boat without food or water; slipping over the line in disguise as priests, peddlers, or peasants, or even fighting one's way through. Truly, none of it appealed to him as making sense just then. Later, the watch on the borders would be less rigorous. To wait discreetly, would not that be the better part of wisdom? Would not the Lord be better served by live worshipers in secret than by a dead one or one driven insane in a dungeon?

Not that he could not endure a dungeon as well as the next one, he assured himself, but what kindness would it be to drag Madeleine from the comparative safety she now enjoyed and expose her anew to a convent? She would never be permitted a second escape. Suppose they were apprehended together and his part in her first escape became known. Might not he be devoted to the wheel, rather than the galley? In spite of what they said about galleys, he thought he would prefer them to the painful certainty of the wheel. There was something so final about having one's limbs broken by the iron bar! When nursing such thoughts, he would ride in a cold sweat for miles.

He found himself entertaining the thought at times that a marriage without a dowry was not a particularly intelligent venture. Perhaps he had been misled, and recent changes in the fortunes of the Cortots were a divine leading he should not ignore. By the time he had reached the gates of Hauterive, he had come to some decisions.

Mathieu followed the porter to the main entrance of the modest chateau. It stood in the midst of ambitious formal gardens.

"Madame is not here today," the majordomo informed him, eyeing his bedraggled raiment with unconcealed suspicion. Mathieu took the news with admirable fortitude and studied several prints of saints and an apotheosis of Louis XIV on the walls of the antechamber while the servant sought Mademoiselle Cortot.

A door opened behind him and he wheeled to greet his promised one. He fell to his knees and kissed her hand fervently. Her eyes glowed with excitement. Standing silently and feasting his eyes on the familiar beauty of her face, his troubling thoughts vanished like smoke. He became aware that she was speaking, and her warm, low voice brought back such memories that once again he felt all courage and devotion.

"You look so fatigued, Mathieu. There's hollowness about your eyes. It has been a hard journey? I am so glad you've come at last. And my father? How did you leave him? Where is he living? He hasn't answered my last letters. Do you bring word from him?"

"I do," he whispered, and looked questioningly about the white paneled room, especially at the open door into the hall.

"It's beautiful outside," she responded instantly. "Let's go into the garden. I think the children are out there. They'll be so glad to see you!"

In a moment she reappeared in a flame-colored cloak thrown over her shoulders. It had a peaked hood, but she left her head bare. They went through the French doors and walked slowly up the graveled paths without saying a word. She leaned on his arm, while he gazed solicitously down into her happy face. They put several hedges between them and the house before he began to tell her of his visit to Saint Martin and of her father's instructions. When he had finished, Madeleine had turned white.

"I had no idea matters had come to such a pass," she said, almost in a whisper. "He has written but once since Mother died, but we did not guess from his letter how matters really were. We really ought to go at once to him, but we must do as he wishes. We can be ready any time, dear Mathieu. Cousin Diane has been most kind, but our being here has been a frightful worry to her. If one of the servants should talk, for example! And she's so anxious for her husband's promotion to the *noblesse* of the robe that she'd die if it became known she had heretic kin. She has really been most patient.

"Oh! I have a surprise!" she said, suddenly changing the subject. "Alexandre is here!"

Mathieu shuddered, but she went merrily on: "The monks found him too intractable and let him go!"

Mathieu was the pale one now. He could sympathize with the unfortunate monks.

"It will be good to be *doing* something again," Madeleine went on. "For months it has been the same—up at six and housework or entertaining the children until family prayers at ten in the evening. I have embroidered until I am cross-eyed. And those youngsters! I have hunted the slipper, hid and seeked, loved my love with an A, and read Lafontaine's fables aloud until I have them all mixed up in my sleep. In revenge, I have made Louis and Louise learn most of the Psalms and much of the long and short catechisms. Since Alexandre has come, I've played a little chess with him, but we are indifferent at it. You should have been here, Mathieu. He has forgotten his Latin in shocking fashion. We are bored with these woods and this weather. Truly you are a welcome sight! Let's go into the house, and when Cousin Diane returns we will give her the news."

She suddenly noticed Mathieu's stony face and halted, surprised. "Whatever is the matter, Mathieu? You look like a thundercloud!"

He sucked in a deep breath. Now was the time.

"It appears to me, Madeleine, my dear, that it would be best for the twins and Alexandre to tarry here a season." He saw her mouth open in instant protest. He hastily plunged on with his speech, avoiding her eyes.

"Now, it stands to reason that it is harder for five to pass over the frontier than two. A family group attracts more attention and must move more slowly. When children are observed it is assumed immediately that a family is escaping. They will not be in any great danger, but *you* will as long as you remain in France. Alexandre will be able to watch out for them. Of course, at a future time it will doubtless be possible for them to follow us."

Madeleine looked steadily at Mathieu as he made his case. She said nothing immediately, but he felt his heart sink. She apparently regarded him as if he were something strange and unpleasant she had just discovered. He looked briefly into the violet eyes and found it more comfortable to drop his gaze to her intertwined fingers.

"Indeed!" she commented finally. "That was as strange a speech as I have ever heard! And to hear it from you! You should know perfectly well that I would never leave them here. I trust you are saying this as some sort of a pleasantry, though it is a strange time and place to amuse yourself so. If the matter is so difficult, then let us pray and plan the more."

Mathieu had never been much of a humorist, and he was not

joking now. He dug in his mental heels the more solidly, as he relished the discovery that her protests had not overthrown his determination. He spoke again, condescendingly and patiently, but firmly, as to an unreasonable child.

"I could not be responsible for you, Madeleine, if we have the children with us. As I just said, it would make a larger party and draw dangerous attention to us. You cannot risk being captured a second time. There would be dangers enough for the two of us, but twins are easily recognized, so all perils would be multiplied. You know I would never suggest such a course unless it were absolutely necessary. Trust my judgment, Madeleine. We will not be abandoning them at all. We merely plan that they shall follow later when times are better."

The more he talked, the more persuasive he felt he sounded. Madeleine was facing him with her fists clenched at her sides. She appeared to be struggling for self-control. Her eyes blazed and her lips trembled. For an instant he feared she might burst into tears, and he steeled himself to remain firm. When she found her voice, it was steady enough.

"Monsieur Bertrand. I am indeed surprised at this unworthy proposal. You do not seem to jest, but the idea is preposterous. I have no intention of leaving my brothers and my sister behind as prey for the papists. It appears that I am all they have left in this world. They may indeed come to some sorry pass, but it will not be because I stole off to safety and abandoned them to make their way alone! No, I shall remain here with them."

"Now, mademoiselle!" he expostulated. "You are not using your reason. They would come later. It would increase the chance of success for us all."

"What arrangements did you have in mind for 'later'?"

"Well, that would have to be determined according to the circumstances at the time. You can hardly—"

"No! I stand by what I have said. I'm not leaving here without them, monsieur. Now, unless you have something different to discuss, I feel I am wasting your valuable time."

"Listen to me," he cried in exasperation, grasping for her hand. "How can you even think of getting away by yourself?"

She fell back a pace and avoided him. She tossed her head defiantly.

"Some have managed it, I am told, and perhaps I may yet find someone with the ingenuity to arrange for my brothers and my sister, too."

His temper was fraying badly under the scorn in her voice.

"Oh, indeed? And who might you have in mind?"

"No one at the moment, monsieur, but I'm willing to wait."

Mathieu's self-control dissolved; the words tumbled out: "That apostate ribbon merchant, that dandy from Versailles, I suppose? That bowing, scraping gallant out of a romance—that salon pimp!"

Madeleine's retort sounded icy rather than agitated. "If, as I suppose, this is your picturesque way of referring to the Sieur de Gandon, I may say that I do not even know where he is. However, I doubt that he would expect me to abandon my own flesh and blood."

"The perfect chevalier, eh?" he cried furiously. "So we must risk mortal dangers so one may make comparisons with this hero of the opera? Perhaps we may expect him later in Holland, this debonair one?"

She turned away abruptly.

"If I am not good enough for you, mademoiselle," he continued hotly, "it is time we understood each other. If you are to prove a dutiful wife, it is time we discovered this, too. I take my leave."

Madeleine turned back with her anger mastered. This time she pulled at his sleeve.

"Mathieu, you are beside yourself. This jealousy is unworthy of you. I've been faithful to you. It is *I* who have waited all these months for word from *you,* which never came. I knew the times were evil and that you were likely in danger, and I've been praying daily that we would soon be reunited. I have not seen or heard from the Sieur de Gandon nor any other. I fear your worries have unhinged you, Mathieu. Be reasonable. How could we be happy together remembering the children left here forlorn and in peril? You should not insist I do a thing like that. Don't we mean any more than that to you? Now let us talk calmly, without this shouting."

"I am *quite* reasonable, mademoiselle. You will not reconsider?"

"No, I can't. Don't ask me to, Mathieu." He pushed her hand away, but from the expression on her face, he might as well have struck her.

"Then all I have to say is that your blood be upon your own head, mademoiselle. Good-bye!"

He bowed low, very formally, and turned away, wrapping his cloak about him. He walked slowly, his head held proudly, his boots crunching loudly on the cinders of the pathway. He half expected to hear her call him back. Her tone had been pleading, almost despairing. That was encouraging. Perhaps she was beginning to realize what she was doing. She was just a spoiled child who had always had her own way. But as he approached the iron grille at the end of the garden she had still spoken no word.

As Mathieu reached the gate, he found the twins and Alexandre staring at him round-eyed. Alexandre, he of the missing teeth, gave tongue.

"Hey!" he cried in that piercing tone which brought back so many unhappy memories of the schoolroom at Saint Martin. "If it isn't the master himself! Have you and her highness had a spat? What's going on? We couldn't hear all of it."

Mathieu pushed by them brusquely. Behind him he heard Madeleine's voice, chilly and authoritive:

"That's enough from you, sir. If Monsieur Bertrand wishes his horse, see that Gervais brings it to him at once."

A few moments later, feeling spent and somewhat ill, Mathieu found himself again astride his miserable white horse and moving down the avenue toward the highway. He was outside the gate before he remembered the money belt, and that he had forgotten to say a word about it to Madeleine.

V

FOR three days Mathieu wrestled with his thoughts. His horse plodded obediently eastward, for his tentative destination was Strasbourg, the new French bridgehead on the Rhine. If he could reach that city, adjoined as it was still with the princely states of the Holy Roman Empire, it should not prove too difficult to slip across to safety.

But this was not his immediate worry. He debated endlessly whether he should return to Hauterive. Would not this be tantamount to surrender? Would it not give Madeleine the idea that any whim of hers would rule him? The more he thought of leading a familial parade through the frontier zone, the more clearly he realized how sound his judgment had been. The emotions of a woman, yes, a young girl, were no sound basis for action. To go with all those children—unpredictable, fidgety, irreverent—preposterous! He felt a positive relief to be quit of the whole affair.

But when he recalled how he had allowed himself to become irritable and how, in particular, he had been goaded into blurting out that remark about Gandon, his skin crawled with shame. It was frightful the way that fellow seemed to be hovering over his shoulder all the time. Having seen Armand at his quixotic escapades, Madeleine seemed to expect *him*, Mathieu Bertrand, to be as giddy. Even if she never laid eyes on Gandon again, no doubt she would always be judging her husband by him. She was probably spoiled now to the point where she could not properly appreciate sense and discretion. It was well he had been firm. If she had prevailed, what a wormlike existence he would have led! Perhaps this quarrel was a providential leading.

But then there was the matter of the money. It was not his, and he had no intention of considering it so. Yet what should he do with it? He could hardly make the long journey back across France to Saint Martin. It would be somewhat difficult to explain the situation to Cortot anyway. Perhaps after he had escaped into the Germanies or found his uncle in the Netherlands, he could hire professional guides to rescue the Cortot children. Of course, 300 livres would hardly stretch that far, and a number of things might go wrong with such a scheme. Should he retrace his steps right now? If she were still obdurate, he could always leave the money with her and she could use it as she wished. But there was always the risk that she might overwhelm him with tears and entreaties. He decided not to turn about just yet. It was growing late, and he was very tired. He would spend the night at an inn in the next village and think the matter through once again when he was rested. Surely the border could not be far now.

His mind had been so busy that he scarcely noticed the four nondescript mounted men under a bare-limbed tree some distance from the road. Not until he had passed them did he suddenly discover he was no longer alone. The sudden disappearance of the sun behind the Alsatian hills was not the only reason for the chill that shot through him. The horsemen drew up beside him. His horrified thought was that they were highwaymen, but a quick glance at their arms and accouterments told him that it was worse, if possible.

One rascal, with a single malevolent eye, evidently a brigadier of cavalry, put his gloved hand on Mathieu's bridle.

"Where away, my fine fellow?"

"To visit my—my cousin in Strasbourg," Mathieu gulped feebly.

"Now, how about that?" jeered the soldier. "It has a cousin in Strasbourg!" He turned to his companions and winked. "It has the plumage of a psalm singer, too. A coincidence, no doubt."

Mathieu's heart stopped beating; his viscera knotted in sudden agony. He had no passport or other document, and he was carrying three hundred livres in coin. The injustice of it all, that he should be in such a ghastly predicament through no choice of his own, robbed him of speech.

"Well," observed the noncommissioned officer with another triumphant wink, this time at his victim, "let's go see about this. We have ways of making birds sing, even such molting specimens as thou. I think I know a songbird when I see one!"

VI

DINNER was over. The table had been cleared, and the servants had left Armand alone with the Duc de Lauzières. Neither said much for a time. The dark reaches of the duke's apartment were lit sporadically by the writhing flames in the fireplace. If they reminded Armand of the discomforts of a soul in torment, it was because he felt a similar unease himself. The wood hissed and spat, and the shadows reflected in the mirror over the mantel lent a curious effect to the figurines standing there, as if they were dancing in the uncertain glow.

During the dessert Armand had advanced the hesitant suggestion, the possibility that he might find it advisable to resign his commission and withdraw from the service. The old man had said nothing, and in the eloquent silence Armand had not enlarged on his proposal. The duke had been more friendly and fatherly than ever of late. It was clear what *he* counted on. But nothing would be gained by waiting longer. Armand must find the words tonight.

The duke, almost hidden in his high-backed armchair, sat facing his protegé, his hands resting on the gilded chair arms. The most visible portion of his anatomy was his gouty leg on a brocaded footstool, thrust toward the fire.

"I am flattered that you prefer my company to the charming Princess of Lorraine," he said apropos of nothing. He always sounded a little sarcastic.

"Perhaps it is because you have better manners, my lord."

"Pray don't count on my restraint," returned the duke acidly.

Again they sat silently, the officer gathering his courage and rehearsing his arguments. The clock at the center of the mantel struck the hour.

Suddenly the duke cleared his throat and began to speak. His usually nasal tone was curiously softened, and as he gazed into the fire, it was as if he talked to himself, unaware of a listener in the room. Armand sat with head bowed, his legs crossed, staring at the flames also.

"There was once a young man, the only son of his father," mused the duke, "and heir to one of the oldest and proudest houses of France. He was a youth of great promise, handsome, devoted, brave, and endowed by admiring nature with all the gifts of body and spirit usually distributed among mortals in stingy fashion. The gods themselves must have been jealous, for on an autumn afternoon several years ago, this golden youth rode with his father at the head of the regiment he would one day inherit. A large force of the enemy surprised the column, and in a moment he lay torn and dead, his blood soaking into the thirsty German soil like that of scores of his comrades and most of the superior officers.

"Then it was that another young man, also of ancient lineage but of humbler station, sprang forth from an infantry company, formed a battle line, beat off attacks by the enemy horse, inspiring his men by his steadiness, and led the attack which recaptured the banners of the regiment and not only saved the day but also saved the honor of the distraught father.

"It was fitting that this young man should have been promoted, and indeed he was. But as he observed the competence and formed an appreciation of the character of this young man, who never presumed on his good fortune, an idea formed in the mind of the bereaved father-colonel, an idea which this excellent young man must surely have fathomed by now."

Armand said nothing, nor did he look at the speaker.

"This young man, of whom I speak, has had some doubts, perhaps. But surely he has realized what is open before him as the son of a duke? An adopted son, yes. A colonelcy worth twenty years of his major's pay is but the start, a bagatelle! Glory, standards to take, fortresses to storm, and down the road a few years a marshal's baton! His Majesty would graciously consent to a patent for a title. In the peerage one day, in the inner circle about the royal sun, with the reversion in due time of the titles and offices of the 'parent.' Where need one stop?

"Would some resent an 'interloper'? Only distant kinsmen, witless buffoons with the virtues of their lineage bred out of them, without credit at court and with no teeth to bite."

"I wonder," mused Armand silently, "would I in time also become a 'buffoon' or, in the miasma of the Court, breed buffoons myself?"

"Now what might make such a favored young man restless? Almost certainly there is a petticoat mixed in somewhere. One needs remember that such affairs have a way of turning out differently than one expects. A match could always be arranged with a suitable family —not a difficult matter as the young man's prospects become known."

The duke leaned forward and sought the younger man's eye.

"Nor need one fret about the past," he continued. "No one is excited these days if a Huguenot officer makes an accommodation to the present situation. Take Marshal Turenne as an example. The past slips unobtrusively into the shadows. The Court and the army are full of such discreet ones. No one demands a change in one's mind—just a decent show of devotion to the king's church. If the body is conveyed to chapel, who asks the whereabouts of the mind?

"The prince's religion should be that of all respectable men. If the king is *devot*, then all gentlemen should be *devot*. If the king is atheist, then let all his courtiers be atheist. But for the tranquillity of the state, church and government must support one another. One must learn to sing a litany or to gamble with equal fervor and adroitness. Louis XIV has missed mass just once so far in his life. That is the cue!"

Armand stirred uneasily and seemed about to speak.

"Now, as I say," the duke resumed, "one may believe as one likes. There is nothing too serious in the past of this young man of whom I speak, nothing that cannot be glossed over by his military record. That rescue from the convent was just a youthful peccadillo."

Armand started violently. "How did he find out about that?" he asked himself in consternation.

"These are good days for New Catholics. It rains rewards for those who make graceful submission. For fanatics—only trouble." The duke's voice became urgent. "An exile's life is bitter, my son."

They sat in silence again. Armand's rehearsed speeches had come apart before he could use them, but he could still recall the verse, "What shall it profit a man, if he shall gain the whole world, and lose his own soul?" But what duty did he owe his father's religion? Could he live the sham the duke suggested? So many did. Must one be a fool to be virtuous? Yet it would be a hard thing to walk with the Lord and go hand in hand with the persecutors of His people.

Before Armand's eyes passed visions of the regiment which for so long had been his life. Camped, perhaps by a country roadside, arms and banners stacked, the soldiers about the fires, the pots bubbling, and the aroma of garlic hovering like a benediction as the trumpet notes died away in the twilight. And there were those rare but supreme moments when one shared the intoxication of victory, and drums rolled and banners flew white and free, their brilliant quarterings gleaming in the sun over serried lines blazing with red and blue, gold and steel. Trade this for the life of a hunted fugitive, grubbing for charity among foreigners? He sighed.

"My lord, I thank you for the parable of this young man. I pray you not to inquire closely, for I am not at liberty to tell of a matter I must attend to. But it were better I did not belong to your regiment while it is done. Fool I may be, and, in fact, most certainly am, but I must answer to myself. You were always more considerate than I have deserved, and I would that you could find one more worthy of your great kindness."

"See! I grant you the leave you require before you ask for it," exclaimed the old man, shaking his head gently. "What could be fairer than that? Do what you must, but come back. Then ask for 'instruction'—that's just a word to pacify simpletons. It will smooth your way, and we can forget the jots and tittles of doctrine. Take three months—take a year, if need be—and then report to me again."

Armand's heart smote him.

"My lord," he said haltingly. "I have not been a good exemplar of my faith, but even so, it is not something I could wear hidden guiltily under my coat. I fear that to ask for 'instruction' would be a commitment to be 'converted.' I cannot do this, but I will accept the leave you offer me so kindly, and I will endeavor to be prudent.

105

But, my lord, I beg you, do not strain your great credit with the king trying to save a disobedient soldier—an ingrate. You know that is one thing His Majesty cannot abide. I feel I must obey a Higher Power, but the king will never see it that way."

Armand rose uncertainly. His words had been firm enough, but he knew a guilty relief that his decision did not have to be irrevocable. The door was still slightly ajar, and would remain so as long as the duke could manage it. The old man would never quite understand a sacrifice for religious faith, or a young man's voluntarily leaving Versailles behind.

The soldier knelt and kissed the withered hand of his benefactor.

"If I do not see you again, my lord, I shall always remember your kindness and what you have sought to do for me. Your devoted servant, sire, always."

The old duke sat with bowed head without speaking. Armand crossed to the door, paused with his hand on the knob, bowed deeply, and let himself quietly out.

VII

WITH his decision made, Armand wrapped himself in his riding cloak, checked his pistols, and set out on foot for his destination, the house of the old deacon from whom he must get the passport. The duke's town house was near the Luxembourg, and it was necessary to cross the Pont Neuf. Armand had always found it comforting when crossing that bridge to see the gallant equestrian figure of Henry IV overlooking the Seine. But tonight, as he trudged along the pavement, unbidden thoughts came to mind —that the Protestant hero himself had found it necessary to take "instruction" and for good and sufficient reason had changed his faith. All around the base of the statue, on the point of the Ile de la Cité, were shapeless bundles, barely discernible in the poor light. They were the legless, the blind, the scabrous beggars. He wondered where he might be sleeping on some future night, and a persistent voice told him to turn about and go back to the duke while he still could. He argued with the voice while his legs did their duty and advanced toward his destination.

The old man Armand sought lived near the Tripe Market, not far from the Rue des Sevres. It was a dark trip, and the night was

106

full of rustlings and stirrings. Especially as he walked under the covered gallery between the Pont au Change and the Pont Notre Dame, he kept a hand on his sword hilt and kept away from walls and the mouths of alleys. The noises were usually rats after refuse, but he met some human scavengers, too. They were an ill-favored lot, but gave him a wide berth. A man of his size did not promise easy pickings.

At last he found the little lane he sought. No one was in sight. The buildings rose four and five stories over the street. All were dark, but how many eyes and ears would there be as he tried to rouse the old gentleman at eleven at night?

He knocked softly. The small leaded panes of the windows gleamed eerily in the moonlight. The old man might be dead, gone, or deaf. He knocked more loudly. He was beginning to perspire in the chill night air, when the door slowly opened and a frightened face became dimly visible.

"Who's there?"

"Major de Gandon—you know, from Charenton."

"Come in quickly," the old man whispered, "and not so loud."

Armand followed him down a narrow flight of steps into a little room. It smelled of old food and sour bedding. The host sat on the bed, barely visible in the uncertain light of a candle stump guttering in a dish.

"Forgive my rudeness," said the deacon, rubbing his eyes, "but the night has ears. I have sold my business and will be gone in a week, I hope. I was afraid you might be from the police. One can't be too careful."

"Certainly, I understand," agreed Armand. "I, too, have decided to depart."

"Not so loud," and the old man looked around at the bare walls apprehensively.

"As you said, I'll need a passport and a letter from a bishop," Armand whispered, seating himself on a rickety stool.

"You're just in time then, for I'm having my own made up right now. I can't stand it here any longer. I hope they need shoemakers in Brandenburg, for that's where I'm going." His voice cracked in something almost like a sob. "You know, a week after we were at Charenton, the Edict was revoked and those sons of belial tore down the temple—razed it flat!"

107

"So I heard," Armand nodded. "Now about the passport?"

"So it *was* the last Sunday, just as Pastor Claude said."

"Very true," agreed Armand. "How about the passport?"

"Oh, yes, yes. Now where was it you wished to leave from?"

"From Champagne."

"Then you'll be heading for the Spanish Netherlands. I think that would still be best. They're watching the ports more carefully these days, but it is rough country to the northeast, and winter, too. A good guide should get you across. But be careful, for men's lives are in danger when too many know too much."

Armand nodded grimly.

"I suppose you would do best to coach out through Sedan, but if that is impracticable, you will have to walk. Then ask at the Green Sow for one Rahab. Tell him—now get this—'Our life for yours, if ye utter not this our business.' Tell him Joshua sent you. His name is Baudin, but write none of this down."

"And the passport?"

"I can't take you there, but I'll carry your instructions. Call here in three or four days and I'll have it for you, and a good letter as if by a bishop testifying to your orthodoxy. In fact, in better French than most bishops could command."

"Very good. How much does this come to?"

"Twenty-five *écus** should cover it."

The old man groped for a ragged quill and sharpened it briefly with a penknife. "What are the particulars for the documents?"

Armand looked up at the ceiling for a moment before replying.

"Make the passport to cover Legrand, Anatole, a major, shall we say, on His Majesty's service to the Estates of Holland in the retinue of His Majesty's ambassador, Monsieur d'Avaux."

"Yes."

"The passport will include Madame Legrand and the twins Louis and Louise."

*Coins with a shield (écu) design.

CHAPTER 6

I

"IT WAS very good of you to trouble yourself about us, monsieur," said Madeleine Cortot. Again she stood with a visitor in a corner of the formal garden.

"It would make me very happy to be of service to you, mademoiselle." Armand de Gandon bowed again and shot a glance at the girl's face. Yes, it was thinner, rather grave.

"We had hoped ere this to be in a city of refuge," she replied. "My father has sent us word that we should go on without him, but we do not know where to turn for trustworthy guides. The Gospel says to pray that your flight be not in the winter or on the Sabbath day, and I have hesitated to start out at this time of year with the children."

She glanced at the leaden horizon through the naked trees. The first snows of November would not be long in arriving.

"Mademoiselle has a trustworthy guide for the taking," Armand replied in gentle reproach.

"We could not risk exposing you to the fury of the persecutors again, monsieur." She shook her head firmly. "Once before we—I put you in dreadful peril, but it would not be right to have you risk the galleys now. I didn't realize my father had written you."

He shook his head and started to speak, but she raised her hand.

"It's like your generous nature to wish to help the children of your father's friend, but it is really the responsibility of another."

"Mademoiselle mistakes me," he protested. "I met Pastor Merson several weeks ago at the Charenton temple, and he told me of your father's circumstances. He also told me that Monsieur Bertrand was in the south and that possibly he could not be reunited with you for some time. If, of course, you expect Monsieur Bertrand, I would be happy to give him any assistance I can. I only regret I could not have presented myself at once, but there were matters I had to take care of first."

"I don't expect Monsieur Bertrand," she replied with a peculiar expression, "but that is neither here nor there. It is not right that you again risk your life, your future, and the esteem of your notable friends. Your nature is chivalrous to a fault, but I must refuse to take advantage of it."

She drew the heavy cloak about her more tightly and looked him in the eye.

"It is true," he said, "that I had some silly dreams once, and was fool enough to prattle of them overmuch. But you and your father and the rest of the brethren are my notable friends now. I have said farewell to the others. Believe me, mademoiselle. I have no future in France except as I may help my friends. I would like to be of help to you, if I may."

She bit her lip and dropped her gaze. There were tears on her lashes.

"But, monsieur, what of your regiment, the favor of the king, and all the wonders of Versailles you told me of last spring? Is all this to be sacrificed for a—a *beau geste**?"

"I beg you, mademoiselle, to believe that I speak simple truth. I think I understand better some matters than I did six months ago. Did not Solomon say, 'Better is little with the fear of the Lord than great treasure and trouble therewith'?"

"I wronged you, monsieur," she said softly, but her face was radiant. "It is very good news. We had all hoped for this!"

Neither of them spoke for a while. The wind was rising, whipping the bare branches of the trees outside the garden wall.

"I've been anxious to leave here for a long time," Madeleine said a little later. Her demeanor was more relaxed now. "My poor cousin here has been in torment since the Edict was revoked. She and her husband are trying *so* hard for a title. It would not look well if it were known he had heretics on his premises."

"We'll try to put the good lady's mind at rest speedily." Armand smiled.

"Please understand, she has not asked us to go. But she will be much relieved, I know."

*A fine gesture.

"Let us allow her to think we are going south to rejoin your father. I'm sure she would not intentionally hurt you, but the less she knows the better—is it not so?"

"I have a little money left," she said. "It's not much, for I sent most of what I had left to my father recently. Moïse is not able to work, you know, and my father's health has been none too good."

Armand nodded. "I have a little also, and we'll not use yours unless it's necessary. I'll be able to earn my way more easily over on the other side than a lady will. But what we need now is a plan of campaign. I have a beautiful passport I procured in Paris. It is a veritable work of art, and should permit us, God willing, to pass out in fair comfort by coach as the family of an army officer assigned to our embassy in the Netherlands. I hope," he added hastily, "that you will forgive me for my presumption, but it seemed the best idea at the time. I didn't realize that Alexandre was here with you, but no doubt he can pass as a lackey or the like. If the passport fails, then we shall have to run for it. We may be wallowing in snow soon by the look of that sky! But in any case, I agree with your cousin. This is no place for any of you."

"How much should we tell the children?" Madeleine asked.

"As little as possible until we are on the way. One may hope they are good soldiers? They must realize we are in for an uncomfortable time."

"How soon do you think—"

"As soon as the next coach for the north is due. The longer we wait, the more suspicions will be aroused. Let us not be concerned about baggage."

"We can go any time," she agreed. "The coach for Troyes will pass through the village tomorrow afternoon, if you think we ought to go that way." She glanced toward the house. "Now I think you should come in and meet my cousin. She'll remember you as the one who brought me here last spring, so your arrival will not seem so extraordinary."

Armand offered her his arm. The wind was growing colder and stronger as they strolled up the gravel path.

As he started to open the garden gate, the other three Cortot children materialized from behind a clipped hedge. The twins smiled shyly. Louise, with downcast eye, curtsied to the officer and Louis bobbed a little bow. They were plainly pleased to meet their old friend again, but too embarrassed for speeches. Alexandre grinned from ear to ear.

"Haven't you lost some front teeth since I saw you last?" asked Armand genially. "Was it when you escaped from the House for New Catholics?"

"Escaped indeed!" Alexandre swelled proudly. "I was thrown out!"

"Surely not!" The officer feigned incredulity. He and Madeleine paused by the open gate. She wore the resigned look of one who has heard a story before.

"Oh, they never got far with us. There were about fifty of us in the House, and we encouraged each other. We wore those teachers out. They didn't know what to make of us. We were disorderly at services. We sat crosslegged when we were supposed to kneel. We burnt our devotional books and broke the images of the saints. Then once we pretended to learn our catechism and when they brought in all the devout from the town to show what they had taught us, we gave our own answers! We told them the pope was antichrist and that they worshiped idols and that their church was mystic Babylon, spiritually named Egypt! They got so angry they kicked a dozen of us out."

"Well, they have my sympathy," said Armand with a laugh.

"So then we wandered through the country and spoiled the Egyptians. We knew it wouldn't be good to go home again, so some of the fellows went abroad. But I knew father had thought of sending Madeleine and the twins to Cousin Diane, so I came by to see and here they were!"

"What about your teeth?"

"Oh, them. Well, we were getting pretty ragged on our travels and we were decorating ourselves with clothes from a line in a little village hard by Metz when some of the village chivalry tried to stop us. It's true I got a rock in my face, but it's hardly noticeable now, do you think?"

"Someday, maybe, one might break you in as a musketeer."

"Really! I'm thirteen now. How long would I have to wait?"

"Calm yourself, hero. These are times for craft and cunning. You must obey orders like a good soldier."

"Yes, sir. I will, sir." Alexandre saluted elaborately and fell in behind. The procession approached the chateau.

"This wind cuts right through one," observed Armand. "If the

112

frontier guards are as well frozen as we are likely to be, they may not give us much trouble after all!"

II

COUSIN DIANA bade the Cortots farewell with a decent show of regret. No one volunteered any information about their destination, and she was careful not to ask. She prattled blithely of the pleasant weather to be expected, and the joy of Madeleine's father at their reunion.

The travelers looked like a family of petty nobility accompanied by a servant boy. They made a leisurely progress into Troyes and before dawn the next day took the mail coach for the east.

All that day and most of the next they pitched back and forth in the coach as it crawled up the road to Sedan. Twenty leagues a day was the usual progress, but this trip was not usual. Snow had not yet fallen, but it was bitterly cold.

Madeleine had attired herself in a gray traveling suit, cut similarly to a riding habit, but the cold made it proper for her to wrap up in her red cloak and even hide most of her face. Armand wore a brown suit with little lace and his old gray riding cloak. He also wore a broad-brimmed black hat and a traveling wig, and carried his sword and pistols. Louis and Louise, silent and big-eyed as always, dressed as smaller counterparts of their elders. Alexandre, in raffish glory, rode on the roof, proud and free.

The other passengers offered nothing alarming. A stout merchant, evidently an experienced traveler, had lowered the level in his flask so effectively that he remained virtually insensible to discomfort or to anything else for much of the trip. Two Carmelite nuns sat in the middle of the same seat and their other seatmate was a well-to-do lady of uncertain age returning to Brussels from a visit with her married daughter. She tried at first to make conversation with Madeleine, but Mademoiselle Cortot pleaded indisposition, doubtless genuine enough in the circumstances. So the lady chattered with the sisters of devotional matters, heretics, fashions, herbals, and other such things. On occasion she appealed to Armand as arbiter and he replied good-humoredly, as became a representative of the Parisian *haute monde*.*

*High society.

113

On the second day even the Belgian lady's mill began to run down. A miserable sleet set in, which chilled the passengers to the marrow. The leather curtains of the coach impeded the cold very little. The travelers and the men aloft huddled in their wraps as best they could and endured.

It was becoming evident that this would be one of the last trips of the season; anyone foolish enough to travel after that would have to go horseback. The ruts were frozen hard, and the horses had a difficult time on the slippery road. The coachman endeavored to supply the missing traction with a liberal use of the whip and a constant stream of exhortation to the suffering beasts. On the steeper grades the passengers had to get out and walk. This restored the circulation to some extent, but it made for slow progress.

The stops worried Armand, for any observant loafer or stableboy was another possible link in a chain which might bar their passage at the last minute. He fumed inwardly when they paused for meals or a change of horses. As hour limped after hour and the frontier of the Spanish Netherlands came closer, his spirits began to rise.

Trouble with a coach wheel delayed them the second afternoon, and the party had to put up at the inn in a small town halfway between Montmedy and Sedan. After a discouraging supper, Madeleine and the twins retired to a dank chamber Armand procured for them by a little bribery. They lay huddled together in their cloaks on a bumpy mattress of husks. Armand and Alexandre settled themselves in the common room on a bench against the wall as close to the fire as possible. Alexandre dropped off to sleep instantly, but Armand was still nodding in the unaccustomed warmth and closeness when the optimism he had been permitting himself received a mortal blow. Suddenly he found himself wide awake, listening anxiously.

The coachman, several peasants, and a number of soldiers were restoring their courage and sharpening their intellects at a nearby table. As the liquid precaution against the cold began to take effect, their voices rose.

"They make it well worth your while," one peasant was saying as he hoisted his tankard. "Just last Thursday, Etienne Duclos got thirty-six livres apiece for three of them he caught near Souchard's cow barn. That's thirty-six *each*, mind you. He and his hired man threatened them with pitchforks until they gave up all their money, then they turned them in and got the bounty besides. I call that pretty clever! Etienne won't be sober again, I expect, till after Easter."

"They're under every fallen leaf these days," agreed a little soldier. "No one knows how many slip through, but it'll be less now. The guards at the border are doubled, and they're checking passports more carefully. I don't know where all the forged ones come from, but they'd better be pretty good, I tell you."

"It's spoiled a good thing for the guards," put in his taller companion. "We get changed so often that one hardly has a chance to make arrangements with the guides anymore, or so I hear."

"God's curse on all heretics of course," added the other soldier wistfully, "but it's hard to see how letting a few of them out of the country would hurt much, especially if they left their cash behind."

"If they leave it with honest infantrymen and not with the king's lawyers, you mean?" cackled an old peasant. He found his joke so clever that he had to laugh some more, and continued until he choked and had to be beaten upon the back.

"They won't even be reaching the border as easily as they used to," observed the little soldier when the whooping had finally ceased. "Our patrols run clear back here, and we go as far inside Spanish territory as we wish, until we meet *their* people sometimes. The king of Spain knows better than to complain. And we really sift all travelers passing through Sedan, afoot or horseback or in the coaches. If we have any suspicions, a few days in jail loosens their memories in a wonderful way—especially if you separate a party and question them one by one. The heretics that get through now will have to have special help from their father the devil."

The coachman got up and stretched. "You'd better not delay me. It's getting pretty thick when the mails are held up for such nonsense. As if I don't have trouble enough with these roads!"

He yawned gustily, lurched over to one of the benches muttering, and composed himself for sleep. Then the taller soldier rose.

"It grows late," he said reluctantly, "and I've a long walk back to Sedan. I'm on duty in the morning, and if I'm not on time I might as well be a Calvinist myself. The lieutenant eats them raw. He's just out of cadet school, and I think he has an eye on Louvois's job. He acts like he's the minister of war already."

"Why all the fuss?" yawned a farmer. "Not even a Huguenot would travel in the weather we're going to have before morning."

"That shows *your* ignorance, my man. If it snows, they'll be thick as snow rabbits before you could get through a couple of Pater Nosters. Why, just this afternoon the lieutenant was warned that a family of five of them was heading this way—an officer, his wife, I think it was, and two or three children. A bunch like that ought to be easy to spot. I wouldn't be in their shoes tonight for all the wine in France."

Armand suddenly had trouble breathing. Had Madeleine's cousin reported them or had someone else told on them?

"Wait till the lieutenant runs this coachful through his sieve," the soldier continued with a glance at the snoring coachman. "They'll spend the day sitting right there at the Sedan gate, I'll bet."

The soldier gave his baggy trousers a hitch, wrapped a faded cloak about his shoulders, and opened the door.

"Worse luck! It's snowing!" he cried in dismay, but he plunged out anyway, followed by his short friend.

The party quickly broke up, the others leaving to get home before the snow would be deep. A number of travelers remained, stretched on benches in the common room. The host, seeing his services were no longer required, thriftily drained the rest of the mulled wine, removed his apron, barred the door, blew out the candles, and retired upstairs to his bed.

In time the fire burned low. Armand hunched motionless and pondered the turn of events. The passport, on which he had set such store, was worthless. He made his decision. Rising carefully with his scabbard in his hand for quietness' sake, he took a candle stub from a table and lit it in the embers in the fireplace. Then he shook Alexandre gently and motioned him to follow. As daintily as possible in his heavy boots, he tiptoed across the room, trailed by the wondering Alexandre, up the four or five steps to the door of Madeleine's room. The ill-hung door creaked alarmingly as he opened it. He paused for a moment to listen to the reassuring variety of snores, whistles, and heavy breathing behind them before entering.

For a moment he stood looking down on the sleeping Madeleine. In the dim light all he could see was the curve of her cheek and the long dark lashes, for her head was partially covered. The twins had burrowed out of sight in the pile of covering. Then he realized her eyes had opened and that she was looking at him with apprehension. He leaned over and whispered the bad news. Her eyes widened, but she nodded.

116

"What now?" she murmured with a quick look at the door.

"Before I left Paris," he said softly, "I was told of an inn in Sedan where guides might be obtained. Now if they have not been uncovered yet, this would be our best chance. Certainly better than for me to try to find our way through these woods. Sedan is about a league away. If we follow the road, we ought to be there by morning and all may yet be well. Let's hope the snow will keep the peasants and the patrols indoors."

She carefully roused Louis and Louise while Armand stood there with the guttering candle. He was grateful that they awoke quietly, for in his state of mind, every roach that rustled across the floor, every creak of aged timber, sounded like a cavalry squadron crossing a bridge. The children sat for a moment rubbing their eyes. As he whispered, they did not look at him but stared at his tremendous flickering shadow on the wall and the low ceiling.

"It's snowing, but if we walk along quickly, we shall not be too cold. Remember," he added, "no matter what happens, not a sound!"

They nodded, their eyes enormous. None of the four Cortots questioned his judgment. Armand felt a little awed by such complete confidence.

"Before we start, we should ask the Lord's protection," said Madeleine. The twins knelt by the bed, and Louis recited a short prayer in his solemn way:

"The good child nothing begins
  But he prays to God first.
The perverse child is accustomed
  To do everything without praying to God."

"We'll go out the window," Armand directed. "I'll go first and Alexandre will hand the twins down."

It would have been too risky to take them through the common room and try to unbar the door in the presence of so many sleepers. As the bedroom window was too high to reach from the ground and opened on an interior court, it was not barred. Armand launched himself into the void, praying that there would be nothing dangerous underneath. He landed hard in a rubbish heap and went to his hands and knees. After a moment of testing for anything sprained or broken, he stood erect and hissed at the dark square above. Catching the children was not difficult, but when Madeleine climbed out and dropped, lissome as she was, he thought he had broken his back and perhaps hers too. Once the shock was past, she wriggled free, almost indignantly. In the meantime, Alexandre dropped unassisted.

Taking Louis by the hand, Armand felt his way to the gate, followed by Madeleine and Louise, with Alexandre as rear guard. Muffled by the falling snow, the noise he made fumbling with the catch was hardly audible, and the quintet passed out into the deserted street.

III

THE night went better than Armand had feared. The snowfall, though not heavy, was enough to cover their tracks. They traveled along the edge of the road, ready to take cover if anyone approached. Madeleine's shoes were not made for walking in snow, however, and her skirts became wet and bedraggled. Thanks to the weather, their journey was a solitary one. Just before dawn they approached the town of Sedan, and Armand settled the Cortots behind some bushes several hundred feet from the road, while he set out for town to hunt up the guide.

As he approached the stone gate, he remembered the old deacon's warning against going into towns, but there was no help for it. It was folk fleeing from towns they would be seeking, he reasoned without much conviction. Seizing his chance, Armand strode boldly in the gate beside an ass laden with firewood. The guard did not bat an eye at the gentleman afoot, but pounced on the peasant with the animal. While they haggled over the duty on the wood, Armand slipped out of sight in the narrow streets and began to breathe normally again. He did not wish to ask questions in such a small place nor to loiter about the streets once the citizens were abroad. A few years before, Sedan had been a Huguenot bastion and had a college besides, but then had come apostasy. Now, one could not tell.

Some tramping along the riverbank brought him under the faded wooden sign lettered crudely "The Green Sow." The creature depicted thereon had been blue at one time and the artist's conception of a sow was only indifferently successful.

Not caring to evaluate painting at this time, Armand hesitated outside the door. It was as villainous a place as he had ever seen. The row of houses, of which this cabaret was one, appeared to be leaning upon each other, and it looked as if the one at the end might at any moment be pushed into the Meuse. It was not a place in which a Huguenot would have been seen in normal times. Still, he was more conspicuous standing outside than he would be within.

He pushed the door open and almost strangled in the rancid atmosphere inside. When his eyes adjusted to the dark, he realized he was alone save for the host who was warming his back at a discouraged little blaze in the fireplace.

The two men drank each other in for a long moment. In the light from the fire and the few rays coming through the window-panes, Armand took in the filthy apron, the fishy eye, the face shining with old grease, and a mouth half open and filled with bad teeth. It was not a face to inspire trust. It could have been loved only by an extraordinarily broad-minded mother.

"Monsieur," began Armand with a polite little bow, "perhaps you will do me the service of directing me to Mademoiselle Rahab? I am informed that she may be reached through this inn."

The proprietor scrutinized the visitor unblinkingly.

"Who sent you?"

"Monsieur Joshua."

"Oh? Well, what's he say?"

" 'Our life for yours, if ye utter not this our business.' "

"He's likely to be most anywhere—maybe even out of town," he whined. "I can't be running all over the place looking for him."

Armand divined that an application of the universal remedy was in order, so he fished out one of his precious silver *ecus* and tossed it in his palm. The innkeeper's glance flickered to the coin. Armand flipped it to him. The innkeeper caught it without a word or a smile, bounced it on the counter, and looked it over carefully. Then he put it in his pocket and left abruptly by the back door.

At length the unlovely face reappeared, and Armand was beckoned out the door into an aromatic little alley deep in garbage and frozen slush. They went around a corner and down several steps to a small door set in the masonry foundation of a crazily built wooden tenement. Armand had to stoop to pass through, and he had no sooner started down the damp stone steps when the other slammed the door behind him. For a moment he felt panic in the darkness, but then he realized that a feeble light shone ahead. A few more steps took him down into someone's wine cellar, cold with sweating walls. A small lamp with a burning rag for a wick, as used in the very poorest homes, weakened the darkness. It allowed Armand to find an upended cask to sit on, without letting him see how dirty it was.

He had plenty of time to mull over all the cases of murder and betrayal he had heard of and to marvel at what religion might get one into, when the door opened and a slight, wiry young man about his own age came down the steps. The newcomer had a ferret face and a nervous manner. His clothes told of a clerk or apprentice. He spoke so rapidly, it was hard to understand him.

"Monsieur Rahab?" asked Armand.

"Who sent you?" said the other.

"Monsieur Joshua," said Armand and added the quotation.

"Let us suppose that I am Rahab," said the young man. "What do you want?"

"I understand you travel at times to see kin at Namur. Would you be going again soon?"

"Well?"

"I'd like to accompany you."

"Are you alone?"

"No, I left a woman and three children outside town."

"Rahab" Baudin chewed lightly at his nails. In the dim light it was hard to see his expression, but his tone was hardly encouraging.

"I doubt I'll be going for a time. The weather, you know." He shot a calculating glance at Armand. "It complicates travel."

"How much?"

"Greatly for women, very difficult for children. Accommodations are mediocre, you understand?"

"I quite understand," sighed the soldier. "But assuming the lady and the young persons are experienced travelers, what—or how much—is needed to render the journey, ah, practicable?"

The young man thought this over, perhaps estimating the reduced chances of a group of mixed age and sex in a winter crossing. Doubtless he had seen guides hung in chains when their luck had run out. Armand waited anxiously, for the rates ran from a *pistole** per head on up.

"Two *louis** each," said the guide finally.

Pistole: a coin worth ten livres; *louis*: a gold coin equivalent to four or five dollars.

"The rascal!" Armand thought to himself bitterly. "Two hundred and forty *livres!*"

Haggling was fruitless; Armand had to agree to the sum, though it was twice the going rate. One had to assume that this Rahab was indeed a Rahab and not the Judas he so strongly suggested. All one could do was to pray that he was not one of the breed that led fugitives into traps and then shared the rewards with the soldiery.

"You won't get far prettied up like that," announced Baudin, all business. "I'll bring you clothes that'll fit the part. You have to look like peasants or the game's up before you start."

He mounted the stairs and Armand heard the door close again. He waited as patiently as he could for another hour. Eventually Armand emerged into the weak sunlight in a threadbare gray cloak which covered brown peasant serge. He had reluctantly yielded his suit, cloak, boots, and gloves. When he handed over his wig, he bade good-bye to a two-hundred-livre investment. His bitterest moment came when he had to surrender his sword, his only remaining memento of his father. But he had to agree that a peasant with a sword was a contradiction in terms. In spite of a painful disagreement with Baudin, Armand steadfastly refused to surrender his pistols, arguing that he would carry them concealed. Baudin had profited handsomely enough already. Disposal of Huguenot gear must have been a most profitable sideline for these fellows, Armand concluded morosely.

IV

IT WAS afternoon when Baudin and Armand reached the waiting quartet outside Sedan. While the guide unpacked a bundle of old clothes, the cold, hungry fugitives lunched on black bread, cheese, and melted snow, saving half the loaf for later.

Madeleine did not look overly entranced with the gray peasant blouse and skirt offered her. She said nothing, but made a *moue**** of distaste when she discovered that her garments were not very clean, and a number of small creatures had previously laid claim to them. But Alexandre was frankly enthusiastic about the masquerade, and the twins caught some of his excitement. The guide gathered up

*Grimace.

their good clothing and disappeared toward town, while the refugees strove to perfect their disguises.

Madeleine sniffed. She surveyed the skirt of peasant shortness somewhat doubtfully, and then gingerly began to knot the dingy kerchief under her chin.

"I feel half dressed," she mourned. "This bodice is twice too large."

"There would be no difficulty in making you appear a lady of quality," Armand commented, "but you make a most unconvincing peasant."

He looked alternately at the fine features and the slim ankles. She rocked on her heels to test the wooden shoes, her teeth chattering with the cold.

"Oh, that can be taken care of, I think." She stooped and pried at the frozen ground with a stick. "A little more dirt on the face and hands and perhaps some scratches." She began to apply the dirt like a cosmetic. The twins watched with interest, then imitated her.

"I don't know," said Armand critically. "You're going to have to stoop a little and look more broken-spirited to convince anyone. What is good carriage for a lady is insolence in a milkmaid. See if you can learn to waddle—no, you are not endowed properly for that—shamble, perhaps?"

Under his stare, she blushed and turned away impatiently.

"You might look at yourself," she retorted. "You'll have to do better at Jacques Bonhomme. Right now you look like an officer in disguise—rather poorly done at that. You've got an aristocratic beak that doesn't hide well; you have shaved too recently; and your spine is all parade ground."

He shrugged amiably and refused to argue further.

"I wonder what is keeping our profiteer," he said. "I think I'll take a look out by the road."

Alexandre had been following the conversation closely.

"You know," he said to Madeleine in a low voice, "this should be the test! If you can snare him looking like that, then it's true love."

"You hold your tongue, you loathsome boy," she hissed between clenched teeth. "You're not even to *think* such things."

"And I can add two and two!" he hissed back, mimicking her.

"You are absolutely insufferable!"

"And you are so beautiful when you are angry!"

Armand returned at that moment. "Our Rahab approaches," he said cheerfully. "We'll let him judge our masquerade. It's his neck, too, if the disguise is not a good one. He must know his business or he had been hung long ago!"

V

THEY did not go far that afternoon. The sun disappeared early behind clouds and refused to come back. Obviously more snow was on the way. The guide conducted them to a stone barn at the edge of the hamlet of Floing, about a mile from Sedan, where the travelers spent a snug night in a haymow. Half a dozen other fugitives hid there, too, but they had little opportunity for visiting.

Well before dawn several guides appeared and led their charges off into the dark. As they trudged through the trees, Armand and his party found themselves wondering who the other fugitives were, where they had come from, and what their experiences might have been. Except for murmured greetings, there had been no talk. They wondered especially about one man who had coughed uncontrollably most of the night. As they left, they had paused for prayer. The guide had stood aloof, perhaps offended at an appeal to a Competitor.

The officer and Alexandre would have had no great trouble in keeping up with the guide, but with Madeleine and the twins it was difficult. Baudin had discouraged conversation and throughout the day he seemed to become more sullen than ever. By midafternoon it began to snow again, and travel became harder. Much of the route led up and down rough, forested slopes. When the youngsters began to falter, Armand carried them by turns on his shoulders. Alexandre spelled him manfully, but he could not carry them for as long a time. Madeleine had not said a word for hours, but she was beginning to breath in gasps and to find her wet skirts increasingly an encumbrance. The guide, however, permitted no stops. He seemed to think they should cover the ground as nimbly as he.

The party avoided roads and cut through the forest of Mazarin and the King's Forest by almost invisible trails. At one point they crossed the River Semoy in a leaky rowboat. This put them in or near Spanish territory, but they would not be safe yet, considering how often the French violated the border.

123

About dusk, Armand could stand it no longer. He did not wish to handicap the guide, but they could not continue at this pace. He called for a halt. He was positive the guide heard him but took no notice. The next time, the officer snapped his request as an order. The guide stopped about twenty feet away and half turned.

"A little rest, I beg you, for the sake of the young ones," said Armand.

"I thought monsieur was in haste." His attitude was ugly. Armand fought down a hot retort. "We need him," he reminded himself, "and he does not need us. He has some right to be touchy."

"Certainly," he replied evenly, "but the little ones are exhausted, and we shall make better time for a quarter of an hour's rest."

The guide grunted and his glance wavered between Armand and Madeleine. "For two sous he'd leave us in the lurch," thought Armand grimly, "and for five he'd whistle up the troopers. For all I know, he's been leading us in circles all afternoon."

In the meantime, the four Cortots had sunk down in the snow a third of the way down a steep slope. Below them scattered small trees and bushes cut off the view from down the hill. At the bottom wound a narrow trail, visible from where the guide stood. There was no screen of growth directly below him.

Baudin stood there, one hand in his coat pocket, one leg bent to steady himself on the slope, watching the fugitives silently. It was getting too dark to see his face clearly. Suddenly the man turned his head, and then Armand heard it too. There were voices on the trail. With one accord they looked downhill. From where he crouched, Armand could see nothing, but he could hear the murmuring of men's voices and the muffled jingle of harness. It was a cavalry patrol.

The guide must have felt exposed, though in that dim light his figure would have been hard to distinguish from a bush, even had anyone below thought to look up that way. Perhaps some other idea crossed his mind. In any case, he leaped suddenly away from the refugees and started to run across the opening toward the shrubbery a dozen yards away.

One of the horsemen shouted and almost immediately came the dull report of a carbine. Monsieur Baudin seemed to pause in mid-leap, spun halfway around with his mouth gaping open, folded up, and rolled down the slope.

124

Armand sat for a long moment, his jaw dropped in sheer incredulity at the unlikely shot in that light and distance. Madeleine and Alexandre stared in horror. The twins lying in the snow were too exhausted to know what had happened.

Suddenly gathering his frozen wits, Armand grabbed Madeleine's wrist and dragged her to her feet. He then scooped one child from the snow and Alexandre scrambled for the other. They shuffled desperately up the slope in the direction from which they had come. The men at the foot of the grade were doubtless dismounted by now and would be climbing up to investigate. If the little party could get out of sight, the deepening darkness would cover their footprints for now, and the falling snow would complete the job during the night. Soon they were over the top and panting down the other side.

It was now completely dark and they were lost. Armand decided it would be useless to blunder about in the blackness. They had to have rest, and he would need sunlight or at least daylight to guess in which direction to go.

They hollowed out the snow under the low, overhanging boughs of a huge evergreen. The snowing stopped after a while and it seemed to get colder. Huddling together for warmth under the two cloaks they still had, they spent a night of fitful dozing. The children were tired enough to lie there and peacefully freeze, but Armand insisted that everyone be awakened at intervals to rub feet and hands.

Conversation on such occasions was desultory and wandering. They discussed their late guide and speculated about his intentions, uncertain whether to regard him with pity or to see in his fate divine retribution. Once Madeleine began to search about in distress. She had lost her miniature psalter, and this seemed to upset her particularly for it had been a gift at her first Communion. It was the first and only time on the journey Armand heard her cry. Howling wolves brought them to consciousness twice.

When fatigue threatened to overcome them entirely, Madeleine kept the younger ones awake by putting them through the Ten Commandments, the Apostles' Creed, the Little Catechism, and assorted prayers for special occasions. It was hard work, for her charges were sleepy and resentful. Armand dozed, coming up every so often and hearing the soft murmur of voices in a dark dream world.

"Now recite the 'Mirror of Youth' from the *Christian A B C*,"

125

ordered Madeleine. Alexandre yawned and mumbled haltingly:

> "The good child fears the Lord
> In reverence and all honor.
> The perverse child fears not God
> And nothing does without constraint."

He faltered.
"Good, good. Go on."

> "The good child fears anything to do
> Which might God displease.
> The lax one always himself will plunge
> In dishonesty and lies.

"I've forgotten how the rest of it goes, and I don't see what difference it makes anyway," he grumbled.

"You *do* have it mixed up," his sister replied with a patient yawn.
"That part about the 'lax' goes somewhere else."

She prodded Louis and started him on the second verse. He
recited purely by rote and so faintly Armand could barely hear him:

> "The good child fears anything to do
> Which might God displease.
> The perverse child in all he does,
> Wishes only his own will to do."

VI

VOICES wakened the fugitives soon after
dawn. Through the branches they watched a long single file of foot
soldiers climb slowly up past them. The men were clad mostly in
civilian clothes, almost in rags in some cases, but their bandoliers and
pikes or muskets identified them as infantrymen. They were moving
reluctantly, grumbling as they plowed through the soft snow. They
looked, thought Armand, like men who had not had their breakfast.
The lieutenant, a serious-faced stripling in full uniform, was climbing at the right of the line. The stick he was swinging hit a branch
of the tree under which his quarry was hidden and a small cascade
of snow fell on the breathless watchers below. The officer and the
line padded on, accompanied by aureoles of steam from their labored
breathing. In spite of the grave danger, Armand could not help

smiling. Not too many years had passed since he had been a new lieutenant and much of the world's burdens had rested on *his* shoulders.

The hidden ones had just expelled their breath in relief when they suddenly tensed in horror. Two men at the end of the line had been dropping farther and farther back. Unseen by the sergeant at left rear, they slipped unobtrusively over to a snow-covered log not ten feet from the Huguenots and sat down. The older man laid his pike in the snow, the other leaned his musket against the log, muzzle uppermost. They sat for a few moments beating their blue hands together while the younger one with sincerity and thoroughness gave his views on the army, the sergeant, the lieutenant, the Huguenots, and the weather. His companion remained calm, cracking his knuckles and blowing on his hands.

"It may be warmer where you came from, my young friend," he said reprovingly, "but I think it's going to be a good bit warmer yet where you're going!"

The young soldier glared at his companion.

"At least in Montpellier they're not idiotic enough to chase themselves through the woods on an empty stomach! That dog's head of a lieutenant! He takes it as a personal insult those heretics disappeared last night."

"Maybe they were witches," grunted the other.

"Well, they weren't witches that Baudin fellow was with when he got shot! He wasn't out running around in the snow for his health —not at that time of night, with a pocket full of gold. Everybody along the border knew he was guiding P.R.R.'s—" He swung his arms angrily. "What a miserable business! If I ever see that recruiter who told me all those lies about the army, I'll cut his throat! Up before dawn. Not a chance for a bite or a swallow of something warm."

Madeleine pressed her upper lip, fighting desperately against a sneeze.

"It's all stupid anyway," the young man concluded. "This isn't what I enlisted for." His senior yawned and stretched.

"That's where you're wrong, my boy. Take the word of one who was a soldier when you were still in dresses. It's not for you to say what you enlisted for. If it's the pleasure of His Gracious Majesty that you are to be shot by some Dutchman in the Low Countries while wading in muck up to your elbows, then that's what you enlisted for. If, on the other hand, His Majesty has been seeing less of Louvois and more of the bishops and of Madame de Maintenon, why, then you enlisted to beat the bushes for those who don't go to the right church. It's as simple as that. Be calm and reflective, my boy. If I had my choice, I'd take this over that. *This* is cold and we've had nothing to eat since yesterday afternoon, but *that* is wet, and the Dutchmen shoot at you besides. I will therefore overlook the frightening simplicity of your conversation."

"Why don't you hold your jaw?" interrupted the other rudely.

"Listen, my son. Don't always expose your folly and inexperience. Even if you made marshal someday—what a dreadful thought for France—even then you'd find you wouldn't be able to decide what to do with yourself. Even then there'd be someone to help the king make up his mind, so you'd be just as bad off as you are right now, a very homely private soldier with missing buttons and a runny nose."

The younger man favored the philosopher with a frosty regard.

"If you elderly bores fought as well as you talked, we should have had the Lowlands these twelve years and the heretics would have no place to run to."

It was the other's turn to be offended, and they sat in silence for a moment. The younger snapped a brittle twig from a bare bush protruding from the snow and switched it listlessly. Then came a halloo from somewhere up the white slope behind them. Both soldiers turned their heads, looking unhappily at the line of footprints disappearing into the trees.

"Our martial babe has discovered that the expedition is not up to full strength. Even now he asks the good sergeant to count the lambs." The senior soldier rose and brushed caked snow from his coattails. The other picked up his musket.

"There are thirty of us," he said scornfully. "That big ape can't count beyond five. What they've missed is that big red lantern you carry for a nose. It's like a fifth flag for the regiment."

A second yell, more urgent than the first, echoed among the trees.

"It has ever been the fate of wisdom and experience to be sneered at by callow youth," observed the veteran as he began to move, trailing his pike behind him.

"My apologies. Certainly, if promotions were earned in tavern affrays, *you* would have made marshal by now."

128

They trudged away quarreling, slipping in the snow, but the fugitives remained huddled for a long time. Finally they looked at each other somewhat sheepishly, and tense muscles relaxed.

VII

THE next two days there was a sameness to their torment that made it hard to remember what occurred during a particular day. When the feeble sun appeared for a few minutes, Armand tried to set a course for the north. If they could have gone in a straight line, he felt that the border would not prove far away. But all they had was snow, trees, cold, and hunger.

Later they halted at the edge of a small clearing. Ahead was a modest forester's cottage with stable attached. While Armand debated what to do next, the twins flopped in the snow in a stupor. Armand and Alexandre had been carrying them by turns much of the time, but it was increasingly hard to keep mind and will obedient. The white wilderness numbed more than fingers and toes. Madeleine knelt by the youngsters and looked up frightened.

"They can't go any farther this way. They're hardly out of bib and gown. I can't see them starve here in front of my eyes! I'm going to ask for food at that house!"

Armand was equally positive. "We're lost if you do. They'll hold us and call the troopers. Let's not give up now. It *can't* be much farther!"

"Well, one mile or twenty—they can't go on without food."

Armand was stupid with fatigue and hunger himself. He shrugged.

"Perhaps so. Maybe we were led this way for their sakes. If just the children and you— God grant that they are folk with kind hearts."

However, he made them wait until it seemed certain that the man of the house was not in. The afternoon was waning when Madeleine half led and half dragged Louis and Louise to the cottage door, followed by a subdued Alexandre. Armand lay in concealment and watched them.

Madeleine had to knock twice before the door opened an inch and a frightened young peasant woman peeped out. She started to close the door again.

"Please!" Madeleine's voice was so despairing that the woman reluctantly opened the door a little wider. The Cortots entered the

129

single room with its great bed in one corner, the chest in the other, and the fireplace with copper kettles gleaming dully on the wall above. The floor was earthen.

The woman, blond and sturdy, wore plain, threadbare clothing. Three towheaded children clung to her skirts. They looked frightened, too, for they probably saw few strangers in this isolated place. But what instantly drew the attention of the visitors was the iron pot with a vegetable stew bubbling on the hearth. The smell along with the closeness of the room made Madeleine dizzy. The forester's wife noticed her pale face and helped her to a three-legged stool.

"We've been on a journey," Madeleine explained unnecessarily. "I think we have lost our way, and we saw your house among the trees. Could I beg you to feed the children? They are spent. I'll need nothing, if you have but little."

The woman looked uneasily at the door. Her mind was not hard to read. "Her husband is out hunting us right now," Madeleine thought in despair. "Armand was right. I ruined us, but what else was there to do?" Her anguish was so plain, it seemed to help the woman make up her mind.

"You are welcome," she murmured in the local dialect, "but we don't have much to offer." She brushed aside her brood and took down four wooden bowls, filling them with the stew. It was mostly turnip, for such people did not often see meat. But it was hot. She had them sit at the trestle table while she hacked off coarse hunks of blackish bread. Madeleine furtively concealed her piece, thinking of the famished Armand outside in the snow.

With the sudden relaxation and the warmth, Madeleine felt such a lassitude creeping over her that she wished she could lie down and sleep for a century. She looked longingly at the feather bed behind the green serge curtains and wondered if she would ever luxuriate in a real bed again. But they must not tarry and compromise their hostess. Either the woman had decided charity was permissible if one did not know the identity of the guests, or she expected her husband soon.

She firmly refused any money and insisted they take the rest of the loaf. She held the door for them as they filed out into the winter again, and gave them a pitying look as she closed it. Madeleine had, however, left a gold coin under her bowl, and felt that never had she received such value for her money.

VIII

THAT night they spent a little more comfortably, this time in a strawstack. In the morning they struck a forest path and followed in the direction Armand hoped was north. The thick snow showed their prints remorselessly, so they struggled along the roadside, ready to dive for cover if anyone appeared. When sure they were alone, they softly sang some of the psalms of Marot. Again the rests tended to become longer and more frequent. The bread gave out, and courage began to slip.

In the early afternoon, they had one close call when they collided with a cavalry patrol. Armand and Alexandre leaped to shelter, but Madeleine and the twins, lagging a little behind, their hearing dulled by fatigue, did not run in time. The girl had the good sense to keep walking as if indifferent to the horsemen. The trio no doubt looked as gray and ragged as any other peasants, and the bored troopers, wrapped to the nose against the cold, showed no curiosity. Armand held his breath as the soldiers passed, for he knew better than the brave Madeleine what a slug from a carbine could do. Only her tattered rags looked the peasant, he decided. Her carriage was as defiant as ever; she betrayed no peasant in her features.

IX

LATE in the afternoon, coming over a rise, Armand halted dumbfounded. Before the travelers stood a hut, a wooden barrier, and the river flowing by the side of the road. Wooded slopes rose on both sides. It was a French border post. They must have wandered back into France again, perhaps into the finger of land pointing north from Givet.

They sat down behind a tree and held a council. They could cut off into the forest and hills, but then they would lose the road and the river. The children were in no condition to begin that all over again. The Lord had brought them thus far, said Armand, and though by no means as self-confident as he had been a few days earlier, he was for attempting to brazen their way through. This time it was Madeleine who protested.

"We'll see," Armand said. "If the Lord will provide but a single sentinel, and a venal one by preference, all may go well yet."

He stood up and looked down at his charges. Their faces were pinched with hunger and fatigue, their lips blue with cold. Even Alexandre said little.

On the occasion of that battle seven years before, he reminded himself, the odds had been nearly hopeless. If the Imperialist colonel had known his business, Armand and his men would have been picked up in blankets. Now he felt the same dryness in his mouth he had known that day when the enemy horse came bearing down on his wavering company and he realized that the French cavalry on his flank was oozing to the rear. He had done all he could do and left the rest with the Lord. His musketeers had held steady until the moment to fire, and the tide turned. Now again he must hold steady and leave the rest to the Lord.

"You remain where you are," he told the Cortots. "I'm going down and try to persuade the guard to let us through. Let us each have a bundle of sticks as if we had been gathering firewood. If it goes all right, I'll signal you to go through the barrier. Go without stopping, mind you, or saying a word, no matter what I do. If I'm seized, keep your heads. Hide here till dark, then try to go around through the woods and regain the road as soon as you can. The Spanish border must be very close now. Truly, I had thought we were there already. I'll go now and see what the Lord intends for us." Straightening up, he threw them a debonair half salute. Louise began to cry.

Smoke was rising from the guard hut some yards from the road. Sounds of drunken quarreling inside could be heard. The sentry at the barrier was stamping his feet and singing softly to himself a current ditty good for a sentence in any Paris jail:

> "If you want to know why
> La Chaise is the king's confessor,
> It's because this sneaky priest—"

Armand approached, trying to look as humble as possible. The singer stopped abruptly and wheeled on the newcomer. Under the scrutiny of the sentry, Armand attempted to amble peasant-fashion. It was not too difficult, for he felt weak from hunger.

The soldier was short and slight, with bright black eyes set close together. He had missing teeth. His hat brim was folded up on each side, revealing the face of the younger of the two soldiers who had been quarreling in the snow several mornings earlier.

Armand removed his hat and tried to cringe as became a ragged inferior. This was difficult, for the soldier was a head shorter.

"Who goes?" snapped the soldier.

"I'd like to go up the road yonder," replied the bogus peasant hesitantly. "I came down this morning to gather wood and it's shorter home this way. I'm from the village right up the road." "If I were alone," thought Armand, "I'd have a try at clubbing him, for my pistols are surely too wet to fire."

"Well, let's see your passport," demanded the soldier, leaning his arm on the musket barrel.

"Passport? I never needed one before to gather wood!" Armand tried to strike the proper aggrieved note.

"I'll wager you didn't." He elevated the musket until it pointed at Armand's empty stomach. "Now tell me a better one, my boy, or I'll call the guard. The sergeant will know how to make you talk." His voice was still low, and his noisy comrades behind the shut door could have heard nothing.

Armand felt faint and sweaty. With a four-day beard, his rags, and the bundle of sticks, he had hoped for better than this.

"You're a soldier, I'll warrant," accused the sentry without waiting for an answer. "An officer?" There was just a touch of respect or uncertainty creeping in. His eye sought the identifying sash which was not there.

"I am, or was," confessed Armand. "You've spotted me fairly enough. I was major in the Maine Regiment. And you?"

"Vermandois."

"I recall that we fought alongside of you at Langenbruck in '79. Were you there?"

The sentry seemed flattered at being taken for a veteran, but kept his piece leveled.

"No, but I've heard of the affair often enough from the old liars who make up this outfit. Wasn't that the time when one of your lieutenants rallied the whole line and recaptured the flags practically by himself?"

"Yes. I was there and saw it," said Armand truthfully. The sentry whistled softly.

"I wish we might have known each other in such times," Armand added courteously, "but here we are out in the cold with our teeth chattering."

"Yes, I might as well turn you in. No doubt you're a P.R.R.?"

"True, but I wonder if you would first do me a favor, as a man of the Vermandois for a comrade of the Maine?"

The sentry was silent but kept his shrewd eyes on the suppliant.

"I promised a fine old man," continued Armand, "a comrade of my father's at the Battle of the Dunes, that I'd see his daughter and little ones out of this and to their friends in Holland. If you feel you could let four young peasants through with firewood, I'd be honored to accept arrest at your hands."

"What! Don't you want to cross over, too?" The soldier was whispering now.

"Certainly, but you caught me fairly, and I can't complain. But as to tormenting a young lady and children who have already lost their loved ones and goods, well, that isn't what you enlisted for, is it?"

The soldier stared at him queerly but said nothing.

"Since I'll have no further use for it and wouldn't want it spread among those who have done nothing to deserve it, may I present you with this?" With a slight bow, he offered his purse to his captor. The soldier glanced slyly at the hut and quickly hid the purse in his shirt. He lowered the gun.

"Well, send 'em through, but you'd better not go with them. If anyone happened to see five of you, it might remind them of some folks we're supposed to be watching for. Hide here below on the riverbank till it's dark, and I'll give you a chance to go before I'm relieved. But be careful even out there." He pointed north. "The border is back of us here, but our horse wander all over. Who cares for the king of Spain, eh?" He winked in comradely fashion.

Armand started to stammer his thanks, but was silenced with a lordly gesture.

"I don't know why I'm doing this, but you're right. I *didn't* enlist for this. To wear a hat with a feather and be bawled out by flatheaded sergeants? The bastinado if you forget to salute. And this five-sous-a-day freezing in the snow on Madame de Maintenon's business!" His tone was vicious.

"With this—" the soldier patted the purse under his jacket—"I'll buy into a public house back at Montpellier. But go while you can and come and see us down south some day."

Armand waved the Cortots on, then jumped down the bank, where he lay flat in the gravel.

Madeleine and the others moved forward, though mystified at Armand's actions. They hoisted their bundles of sticks and plodded down to the barrier. Armand was not to be seen. As they approached the sentry, he shifted his musket to his left hand and with his right carefully lifted the bar just enough for them to slip through. Madeleine sought his face anxiously, but he was impassive and said not a word. He replaced the barrier swiftly and watched them as they walked hurriedly down the road and around the bend. They dared not turn for a last glance at their native land.

It was about dark when the soldier finally called Armand. He had been lying on the frozen ground so long he thought he could not bend his joints, but he scrambled up to the sentry fast enough.

"You'd better be off, major," he said in a low voice, "but remember, stay separate until you reach a large Belgian town. Have you any money? Perhaps you'd better take back some of this." He reached inside his jacket.

"No, no!" Armand insisted. "I'll get on all right. God bless you for your good heart. Perhaps you'll never make marshal now, but at least you should be a prince of innkeepers." He clasped the hand of the soldier.

Just as he turned to slip by the barrier, he heard the unmistakable sound of horses' hooves from the direction of France. He shot a questioning look at the sentry.

"Will they be riding over the line?"

"Don't worry, major. I'll delay them a little for you."

Without further ado, Armand set off as fast as he could manage without actually running. The soldier watched him go around the bend and out of sight.

X

IN THE dusk the jingling of harness sounded distinctly. The patrol would appear over the rise at any moment.

Suddenly the soldier let out a loud yell and fired his piece in the air. Instantly the door of the hut burst open and a squad of soldiers boiled out, followed by a burly sergeant.

"Two of 'em up the slope there," cried the sentry, pointing back toward France. The sergeant and his men set out on the run and were presently joined by the horsemen. After several confused minutes of checking their own footprints, they all came straggling back.

"Huguenots, bah! There wasn't even a cow up there. I don't know why all the half-wits from every foundling home in France have to be shoveled into this regiment. For this you can do the next turn on duty, too!" The sergeant disappeared into the hut.

The cavalrymen dismounted to warm their hands and to chaff the unlucky sentry. He took it pleasantly enough, though. His gaze was abstracted and far away, like that of a man who fancied himself already established as a prosperous innkeeper.

After half an hour the cavaliers remounted in leisurely fashion and the horses stalked up the snowy road into the land of the king of Spain.